**"You'**

said Tooley. "My tent sleeps two."

"No, thank you," Bolivia replied.

"You could make a poor vet happy."

"You look happy enough to me," she said, seeing him grin. "I enjoyed lunch," she added, getting ready to leave the jungle encampment.

"I can guarantee you'd like the siesta even more," he promised.

For a moment she was half tempted to say, *Get rid of your men, Tooley, and you've got yourself a deal*. The next moment she was saying, "I think it's time for me to hit the road."

She could have sworn, from his final grin, that he'd known exactly what she was thinking.

Dear Reader,

When two people fall in love, the world is suddenly new and exciting, and it's that same excitement we bring to you in Silhouette Intimate Moments. These are stories with scope and grandeur. The characters lead lives we all dream of, and everything they do reflects the wonder of being in love.

Longer and more sensuous than most romances, Silhouette Intimate Moments novels take you away from everyday life and let you share the magic of love. Adventure, glamour, drama, even suspense—these are the passwords that let you into a world where love has a power beyond the ordinary, where the best authors in the field today create stories of love and commitment that will stay with you always.

In coming months look for novels by your favorite authors: Kathleen Creighton, Heather Graham Pozzessere, Nora Roberts and Marilyn Pappano, to name just a few. And whenever you buy books, look for all the Silhouette Intimate Moments, love stories *for* today's woman *by* today's woman.

Leslie J. Wainger
Senior Editor and Editorial Coordinator

# Betrayed
## BEVERLY SOMMERS

Published by Silhouette Books New York
**America's Publisher of Contemporary Romance**

SILHOUETTE BOOKS
300 East 42nd St., New York, N.Y. 10017

Copyright © 1990 by Beverly Sommers

All rights reserved. Except for use in any review, the reproduction or utilization of this work in whole or in part in any form by any electronic, mechanical or other means, now known or hereafter invented, including xerography, photocopying and recording, or in any information storage or retrieval system, is forbidden without the permission of Silhouette Books, 300 E. 42nd St., New York, N.Y. 10017

ISBN: 0-373-07329-1

First Silhouette Books printing April 1990

All the characters in this book are fictitious. Any resemblance to actual persons, living or dead, is purely coincidental.

®: Trademark used under license and registered in the United States Patent and Trademark Office and in other countries.

Printed in the U.S.A.

**Books by Beverly Sommers**

Silhouette Intimate Moments

*Reason to Believe* #164
*\*Accused* #325
*\*Betrayed* #329

\*Friends for Life trilogy

---

## *BEVERLY SOMMERS*

grew up in Evanston, Illinois, and went on to college in California, graduating with a major in English. Subsequently she has studied law, taught fifth grade, been a counselor in Juvenile Hall and owned an art gallery. She has lived in Spain and Greece and currently makes her home in California.

# Chapter 1

She stepped out of the helicopter into the blinding sun of the desert. As far as she could see there was only sand: no buildings, no palm trees, not even a mirage. She turned around in time to see the pilot give her the thumbs up sign before taking the helicopter back up.

Her khaki pants flapped wildly around her legs as the helicopter took off, then gradually they calmed down and she realized she was the only human being within miles. She finally believed she was actually going to do it. It would be the coup of her career.

Then, off to the south, she saw the slightest bit of dust being raised. It was he; it had to be. She shaded her eyes and watched as the dust ball began to grow, signaling the arrival of a vehicle.

As she stood watching the advancing vehicle she heard a noise behind her. She quickly turned to the north and saw, approaching her, an old, battered bus. She looked back to the south. The bus was going to reach her first.

*Feeling dismay, then chagrin and then anger, she realized her exclusive had been blown. The bus pulled up within feet of her, and its doors discharged several dozen members of the press, all of them closing in on her. They surrounded her and then moved past her, running now to the jeep that had pulled up a few yards away.*

*In the driver's seat of the jeep was a familiar figure, his black checked kaffiyeh framing his face. Behind him sat two young men with Uzis.*

*"Chairman Arafat! Chairman Arafat!" everyone was yelling at once.*

*She moved into gear then, shouldering her way through the other reporters and cameramen, her eyes on her target. As she burst through the front ranks of the crowd, she yelled out, "Chairman Arafat, is it true that you're meeting with the Israeli prime minister?"*

*Dark brown eyes turned to stare at her from beneath the kaffiyeh. He blinked once, then stood up in the jeep to get a better look at her.*

*"You!" he shouted.*

*"Me?" she asked, pointing to herself.*

*"Yes," said the Chairman. "Aren't you Bolivia Smith of the* Miami Times*?"*

*"Yes, sir."*

*"Come," said Chairman Arafat, pointing to the passenger seat. "You will join me. I wish to give you an exclusive interview."*

*There were angry grumblings as Bolivia trotted over to the jeep and climbed into the passenger seat. Then, without further ado, Chairman Arafat drove off.*

The knock on the door rudely interrupted her daydream, and before she could yell, "Go away," the door opened and her boss stuck his head in.

"You working on anything?" he asked her.

Bolivia made an abysmal attempt to straighten up in her chair. "Yeah, a few things," she said, hoping that Henry wouldn't ask her to get any more specific.

"I got something you might be interested in."

She tried not to let her enthusiasm show. It was three days until her column was due, though, and she hadn't come up with an idea yet.

Henry came into the office and threw a stack of letters on her desk. Then he walked behind her and pulled open the blinds on her window. The sudden sunlight practically blinded her.

"What are these?" she asked, pulling the first letter.

"Complaints."

"Police corruption?"

Henry shook his head. "No such luck. It seems a bunch of Vietnam vets have a jungle camp pitched not far from a nice suburban neighborhood in Lauderdale."

"Why don't they write the Fort Lauderdale paper?"

"I guess they trust the *Times*."

Bolivia gave a snort of derision.

"Okay, so it's you they trust. Each letter mentions you by name."

Bolivia put down the letter and instead studied the envelopes. "They're all neighbors. It looks as though they got together and did this. Are they form letters?"

"See for yourself. If you're interested, go with it. If not, dump them."

As Henry walked out, Bolivia started to read the first letter. When she had read them all, she noted certain similarities. They were all worried about the vets being in the neighborhood, but one was primarily worried about the possibility of the vets being involved with drugs and the fact that she had a teenage son; another was worried about the young girls in the neighborhood; a third was worried about the property values dropping. Only one claimed to be worried about the vets themselves, wanting to know why the government was letting them go homeless.

Bolivia's weekly investigative column was called What's Happening? and what she liked to investigate was government corruption. If she couldn't find any she would settle for injustice in the criminal courts system. Sometimes she went after minority discrimination. What she didn't like to write about was a bunch of suburban ladies who complained whenever reality intruded on their lives. On the other hand, she didn't have one legitimate idea for her column this week, and at least it would be a nice ride to Lauderdale. Not today, though; she'd go in the morning.

One of Bolivia's objectives in life was to strive for a feeling of impermanency. If she began to feel comfortable, she changed her circumstances; if something began to have a feeling of nostalgia about it, she discarded it; if she inadvertently began to accumulate possessions, she got rid of them. There were only two immutables in her life: her vocation and her two best friends. Even her family kept changing, her mother and father, long divorced, were seemingly in some kind of contest to see who could marry more partners during their lifetime. Bolivia had lost count of her half brothers and half sisters and stepbrothers and stepsisters and everyone else involved.

Because she liked this feeling of nothing being forever, because she kept hoping that one of these days she'd be given a foreign assignment, because she aspired one day to be a bureau chief in some Third World country—preferably one at war—she lived in a hotel. This season the hotel she resided in was The Seventeen Palms, a sleazy pink nonentity in Miami Beach that she could only assume had once seen better days. It had a view of the ocean, but that was a given in Miami Beach. It had the requisite number of palm trees to validate its name. It had, during the season, parties of old people and kosher food in the dining room, and a has-been comic in the bar. Off season, things went steadily down hill. Once the last party of New Yorkers checked out in early April, the air-conditioning had suddenly gone on the blink. Despite protests—written, asked in a polite way, conveyed by her lawyer, and, finally, when all else failed, yelled at the owners in a threatening way—it was now July and it still hadn't been fixed.

July in Miami is very much like living in a laundromat with all the washers and dryers turned on. That's your average July. This year, along with the rest of the country, temperatures were breaking all records for heat. It had gotten so bad people were praying for a hurricane.

Nobody in his right mind visits Miami Beach in the summer. No one in New York says, "Hey, let's go down to Miami to cool off." The state of Maine comes more naturally to mind. People don't say, "Hey, I bet it's cheap down there off-season." It's also cheap in the winter, and that's the only time Miami comes to mind. If you can afford it, you go to the Caribbean; if you can't afford it, you go to Miami. That's the way things are, and the hotel owners, Arthur and Julie, a cutesy couple in the slum landlord mode, weren't unreasonable in assuming that they could save plenty of dough by turning off the air-conditioning after the last of the tourists left. Except that there were still Bolivia and two other permanent residents, none of whom had bargained for the off-season being hot and humid indoors as well as out. The last time Bolivia had asked to speak to the owners, this time with the object of getting her deposit back and moving out, she had been told that they were in Alaska for the summer. Obviously they were smarter than she was.

Bolivia had a few options. She could find a boyfriend with an air-conditioned abode; she could impose on her friends; she could sleep at the office. What she did instead was start to drink a few beers at night, just enough to aid her in falling asleep without noticing that she was sleeping in a pool of sweat. This didn't do much for her mornings, of course. Her hangover's were evolving from slight, but annoying, to somewhere beyond mere annoyance, and she was beginning to wonder if she was going to have to end up blowing her apartment deposit on the Betty Ford Clinic when the summer was over.

Tonight, at least, she'd be drinking with friends. Her softball team had a game scheduled, and afterward she, Sandy and Anne would go out with the rest of the team after the game and have a few beers.

"You're getting *married*?" Bolivia asked Anne in disbelief.

"Yes."

"I don't believe it," said Bolivia. "Do you believe it?" she asked Sandy.

"It's not exactly a surprise," said Sandy, always the diplomat. "I mean, we know they're in love."

"But *marriage*?" asked Bolivia. "Why do you have to marry him?"

"I want to," said Anne.

"Why don't you just move in with him?" asked Bolivia.

Anne exchanged glances with Sandy and then rolled her eyes. "What's the difference?"

"Marriage seems so final," said Bolivia, although where she'd picked up that notion she didn't know. Certainly not from her parents.

"That's what I'm hoping," Anne said.

"I think it's romantic," said Sandy, looking about as unromantic as possible in a baseball uniform, with dirt all over her face from sliding into home plate in the ninth.

"Jack doesn't want to live together," said Anne. "He tried that once, and it didn't exactly work out. He wants to make it legal this time."

Bolivia didn't like the sound of it at all. Anne was getting married, Sandy was placing ads in the personal section in order to meet men...pretty soon she wasn't going to have two best friends anymore. All she was going to have were two married couples who occasionally invited her to dinner. Why did things have to change?

"When are you going to do it?" asked Bolivia, knowing even as she said it that she was starting to whine.

"August twenty-first," said Anne.

"So soon?"

"What are you going to do with your co-op?" Sandy asked Anne.

"Sell it and move into Jack's house."

"You'll never sell it that fast," said Bolivia. "Particularly in the summer."

"It doesn't matter," said Anne.

And, of course, it didn't. Anne made tons of money as a corporate attorney.

"Yeah, well, okay, I'm happy for you," said Bolivia grudgingly.

"You like Jack," Anne reminded her.

"Sure I like Jack. What's not to like?"

"Nothing will change."

"*Everything* will change," said Bolivia.

"He's not kidnapping me," said Anne. "He's marrying me. I'm still allowed out to see my friends."

"You'll be too in love to go out," said Bolivia.

"I'm not going to be any more in love than I am now," said Anne, "and I'm out, aren't I?"

"You've still got me," said Sandy.

"At the rate you're trying to meet men," said Bolivia, "you won't be around much longer, either."

"Judging by the ones I'm meeting, I will," said Sandy.

"The thing is," said Anne, "I'd like both of you to be in the wedding."

There was a moment of silence from their end of the bar, Bolivia breaking the quiet first with, *"Wedding?"*

"You know," said Anne, "it's what people have when they get married."

"Oh, come on, Annie," said Bolivia, "we've always made fun of weddings."

"We have, you know," agreed Sandy.

"My mother will be very disappointed if I don't have a wedding," said Anne.

"So what?" asked Bolivia, and Sandy nodded in agreement.

Anne couldn't meet their eyes as she said, "Jack wants a wedding."

Bolivia looked at Sandy. "Do you believe that?"

"Not for a minute," said Sandy.

"Men never want weddings," said Bolivia.

"None I've ever heard of, anyway," Sandy added.

"Jack's colleagues, and mine, will expect it," said Anne.

Dead silence.

"Okay," she went on, "so I want a gorgeous dress. You know me, I love clothes."

"That sounds a little closer to the truth," said Sandy.

"Can't you just buy a dress and not have a wedding?" Bolivia asked.

"Aren't I allowed one nostalgic moment in my entire life?" asked Anne. "Look, I'm not talking about any big deal. Just a small wedding with a judge to preside."

"I'm not going to be in any wedding," said Bolivia.

"You'll get to meet all the attorneys I work with," said Anne.

Sandy started to look slightly tempted.

"What exactly do you mean by 'in the wedding'?" asked Bolivia.

"I'd like you to be bridesmaids," said Anne in a rather muffled voice.

Bolivia choked on her beer.

"Or dual maids of honor, whatever you prefer to call yourselves," said Anne.

"I prefer to call myself *out of it*," said Bolivia.

"We'd look ridiculous," said Sandy. "We'd look like Mutt and Jeff."

"We would," Bolivia agreed a little too quickly. Not that it wasn't the truth. At five feet ten, she was almost a foot taller then Sandy. "Everyone would laugh at us."

"You'll both look beautiful," said Anne, sounding as though everything had been decided.

Bolivia balked. "Wait a minute, I just had a great idea. You're going to love this, Annie. Why don't you get married on the baseball diamond and we can all be in uniform?"

"Get serious," said Anne.

"That would be pretty unique," Sandy said.

"What's Jack supposed to wear, an umpire's uniform?" asked Anne. "And what about the guests?"

"You could serve hot dogs and beer," said Bolivia, kind of getting into it.

"I am going to be in ivory silk with my grandmother's pearls, and you're going to be in shell pink organza carrying tea roses."

Bolivia made barfing motions over the bar, and even Sandy looked staggered.

"Pink? You wouldn't catch me dead wearing pink," said Bolivia. "I didn't even wear pink when I was a baby."

"Brunettes look wonderful in pink," said Anne.

"Pink is so...babyish," said Sandy. Not that she didn't already look babyish; at thirty-one she was still asked for ID in bars, but cops always like to think they look old and tough.

"Pink's *sweet*," said Bolivia, making the word sound obscene.

"It's supposed to be sweet," said Anne. "You're supposed to look like virgins."

That broke them all up.

Bolivia was still fretting about it when she rode her Kawasaki to Fort Lauderdale the next morning. First of all, she absolutely refused to wear a dress. She didn't own a dress, hadn't in years, and was not going to get stuck with some pink organza monstrosity. Whatever organza was she didn't like the sound of it. Even if she were about to wear a dress, which she wasn't, she was, under no circumstances, going to wear a pair of high heels, which was exactly what Annie would be demanding next. She didn't think she could even *walk* in a pair of heels. Nor was she going to wear some circlet of pink tea roses on her head like some fairy out of *A Midsummer Night's Dream*. My God, what if someone she knew showed up at the wedding? She'd be laughed out of the newspaper business. Sandy could be maid of honor, and Bolivia would assure Annie that she didn't feel slighted in any way. Sandy wore dresses sometimes, or at least skirts, and heels would at least give her some height so that she wouldn't look like a midget next to Annie. Bolivia would show up at the wedding in some kind of pant outfit with sandals, and that would be that. And she'd host a bachelor party for Annie the night before, complete with open bar and some stud jumping out of a cake. But she wasn't going to be in the wedding party. No way. Thank you, but no!

The wind, even at sixty-five miles per hour, was hot and humid. Which meant that when she stopped riding she would probably drop dead of heat exhaustion. Bolivia leaned into the curve exiting I-95 and followed the directions she had to the subdivision on the outskirts of Lauderdale.

It seemed like a quiet area. It would probably be dead quiet once she shut off her motorcycle. They were large homes surrounded by trees and shrubbery. There were kids playing in the streets who waved to her as she went by, and lots of toys up on the lawns. It looked like a good place to live if you had to be married and have children.

She found Pelican Way and made a right, and then immediately saw the site of the problem. The subdivision ended abruptly. On one side of the street there were houses and lawns. On the other side of the street was what looked like the Everglades. In other words, pure jungle. She wondered if it was state-owned property. If not, why hadn't the developers moved in, destroyed it all, made an artificial lake and built more houses? That was what they had done everywhere else she looked.

She pulled up to the curb and turned off the motor. She put her Kawasaki up on its stand and took off her helmet. Underneath, her hair was soaking wet. She ran her fingers through it so it wouldn't be flat against her skull. She took her camera out of the compartment under the seat and hung it around her neck, then walked up to the Cape Cod style house and knocked at the door.

A boy of about twelve answered.

"Is your mom home?" Bolivia asked him.

"Not if you're selling something."

She liked smart-mouthed kids; she had been one herself, Bolivia stepped aside so that he had a clear view of the street. "Do salesmen usually ride motorcyles?" she asked him.

"Is that yours?" he asked, his eyes growing wide.

In answer Bolivia bounced the helmet on her hand.

"I'll get her," said the boy, trying to close the door, but Bolivia stuck her foot inside. No way was she going to miss a chance for some air-conditioning.

She stood in the entry hall while the boy went to get his mother. She heard a voice saying, "You just let her inside?" and then a pretty woman in her thirties came into view wearing a sweatshirt. That really impressed Bolivia. There were only about four days out of the entire year when it was cool enough to wear a sweatshirt, but this woman was able to make it that cool all the time.

"What is it?" the woman asked her.

"Are you Judy Bower?"

"That's right." She was frowning now.

"I'm Bolivia Smith of the *Miami Times*. I got your letter—"

"You're kidding!"

"No. If you'd like to see some identification—"

"You actually came here? Someone actually read our letters?"

"We read all the letters we get, ma'am." And usually laughed over them.

Judy gave her a big smile. "Come out to the kitchen and I'll fix you something to drink."

Bolivia followed her out and accepted a glass of iced tea. When she was seated in a calico breakfast nook, she said, "I came out to investigate the jungle camp you wrote about."

"You don't look anything like your picture," said Judy. "Your hair's much longer in your picture.

Bolivia could feel her wet hair still plastered to her head. She had envisioned a very short, spiky haircut that would be cool in the summer. With the heat, though, and with her motorcycle helmet mashing down the spikes, what she had could conceivably be called a cap of hair, but Annie and Sandy preferred to call it a mess.

"I cut it," said Bolivia.

"I wouldn't have recognized you," said Judy.

"I guess I need a new picture for the paper." The only photograph she had any interest in posing for, though, was a passport photo.

"I love your column," said Judy. "Sometimes I cut it out and send it to my mother in Indiana."

"Thanks," said Bolivia.

"Have you visited the other women?"

"No, you're the first," said Bolivia, noting how this information seemed to please Judy. "Actually, I was hoping you'd tell me how to get to the camp."

"I really don't know," said Judy. "I've never been in there and we don't allow the kids in. There could be alligators in there for all we know. I can tell you where they come out, though."

"They come out?"

"Oh, yes. They're in and out; otherwise we wouldn't know about them."

"Have they done any harm?"

"No, not really. I just wish something could be done for them."

"Some of your neighbors seem to be frightened."

"Well, a couple of times they've been at the garbage cans at night, and once one of them flirted with Joannie Wright. But that girl's a tramp and probably started it. Anyway, they've got the neighborhood in an uproar. All the men who didn't have guns before are out buying them now. I'm just afraid someone's going to end up hurt."

"We're developing a real homeless problem in Miami," said Bolivia.

"Oh, we have a few in Fort Lauderdale, too, but this is different. These men don't beg or anything. The thing is, they wear those camouflage clothes, and they look like they think a war is going to break out any minute. And with the men in the neighborhood all arming themselves, they could be right."

"Have you talked to the police?"

"They don't do anything. They say no crime's been committed. Once it is, though, then it's a little late."

"Could I sit on your cycle?" came an awed voice.

Bolivia looked around and saw Judy's son. "Sure," she said, handing him the helmet. "You can even wear this."

"Thanks," said the boy, grabbing the helmet and running out of the kitchen.

"You ride a motorcycle?" asked Judy.

"Yes."

"You're braver than I am."

Bolivia shrugged modestly. Actually, she loved being considered brave. What she wasn't brave enough to do was get married and settle down in suburbia, but she didn't mention that to Judy.

"Would you like some more iced tea?"

"I wouldn't mind," said Bolivia, willing to spend as much time as she could in this air-conditioned kitchen. It sure as hell wasn't going to be cool in that jungle across the street.

"How about a croissant? I could warm them up in the microwave."

"Well..."

Judy took out the croissants, and Bolivia didn't demur. She wouldn't mind putting something in her stomach. She had been in too much of a hurry for her usual fried eggs that morning.

"Would you mind a personal question?" asked Judy.

"No, go ahead," said Bolivia.

"Well, my neighbors and I were wondering about your name. It's so unusual. For a person, that is."

"My parents were in Bolivia when I was born. I have a brother named Oslo and a sister named Roma, and... well, you get the picture. Mom thought Smith needed enlivening." Bolivia also had a half sister named Great Falls, which she thought was really nasty of her mother.

Judy set out the croissants, and Bolivia dug in. They were warm and flaky and utterly delicious. Maybe she'd get Annie a microwave for a wedding present. She'd have to find out if Jack already had one.

"I don't suppose . . . no, I shouldn't bother you," said Judy.

"What?" asked Bolivia, speaking with her mouth full.

"Would you autograph your column for me?"

This was a first for Bolivia, and she thought about it for a moment before nodding. Judy handed her a copy of last Friday's paper and a pen, and Bolivia got greasy fingerprints on the paper as she signed her name.

"What are you going to do when you find them?" asked Judy.

"There's really nothing I can do except interview them and write it up," said Bolivia. "If they start getting publicity, though, they'll probably move."

Judy nodded. "I saw a special about men like that on television last year. They seem to pick remote spots around the country and just drop out of society."

"I don't believe they harm anyone," said Bolivia.

"Maybe not in the wilderness, but this is hardly remote."

"Well, I'll do what I can," said Bolivia. "I'll tell them they're upsetting the people around here. At the least, I can suggest they find a path that comes out where families aren't living." Bolivia stood up. "Well, I want to thank you for your hospitality."

"I'm sorry Tommy was rude. You wouldn't believe all the door-to-door salesmen we get out here. The minute you move in, everyone's at your door trying to sell you something."

"I guess I could've called first."

"Listen, it was a real pleasure meeting you. For once I'll have something interesting to tell my husband when he gets home."

Bolivia couldn't even conceive of a life where she didn't always have something interesting to tell someone.

As Judy let her outside she called to her son, "Tommy, would you show Ms. Smith where the men come out?"

Tommy couldn't hear her over the motorcycle sound he was making.

"That's okay, I'll ask him," said Bolivia.

When Tommy saw her he jumped off the motorcycle and handed her the helmet. This time she locked it to the seat. "Would you show me where the men come out of the jungle, Tommy?"

"It is a jungle, isn't it?" asked Tommy. "That's what I always call it, but my mom says it's just mangroves."

"It looks like a jungle to me," said Bolivia.

"Me too!"

He crossed the street with her and pointed out a narrow path disappearing into the thick foliage. "Want me to go with you?" he asked.

"Thanks, but I don't think your mother wants you in there. Would you mind watching my cycle for me, though?"

"No, I'd love to," said Tommy, not even saying goodbye in his haste to get back to the Kawasaki.

Bolivia took two steps into the jungle and felt the darkness close around her.

# Chapter 2

As she stepped into the Amazonian rain forest, the sounds of civilization were cut off with the speed of a remote control, and the sounds of the jungle began to close in.

Swarms of insects kept their distance as though knowing they were up against a formidable foe. To her right, cutting their own swath through the wilderness, a column of army ants relentlessly pursued their mission. Parrots cried out from above, and monkeys could be seen swinging from trees to investigate who was invading their home.

The path disintegrated into a solid wall of dense green, dark green, horrid green, a scary shade of green that resulted from too little sunshine. Bolivia took out her machete and began to hack away at the vines that closed in on her and threatened to strangle her.

It was slow going. Sweat poured off her body, leeches stuck to her ankles, sucking at her blood and draining her *energy. Nothing would stop her, though, in her quest to interview Santa Santana, the wily rebel leader who even now was rumored to be planning the capture of the capital city. It would be the coup of her career and nothing could stop her after that.*

A man in olive drab darted across her path several feet ahead, the sound shattering her daydream. "Hey, you!" yelled Bolivia, but he had already disappeared from sight.

"Wait up," she called out, wondering if she had imagined him.

It didn't matter, really. It wasn't as though she were lost. The trail seemed to lead somewhere, and she was sure it was to the jungle camp. She had a feeling he was warning the others she was coming and she didn't like that. Investigative reporters preferred to show up unexpectedly.

She tried to get back into her daydream, but reality kept intruding. Reality—the fact that the newspaper had appointed a new bureau chief in Nicaragua and she hadn't even been a contender. Or the fact that her boss pretended to take her seriously, even gave her her own column, but whenever she mentioned places like Beirut or San Salvador or even Belfast, she was virtually ignored. And the fact that the only reason she had gone into journalism was because she wanted travel and adventure and danger. Not that some wouldn't say that Miami was dangerous enough as it was, but Bolivia longed for war. A real war.

So here she was, wasting her time on some Vietnam vets who had dropped out of society. Big deal. She might not even get a column out of it. Maybe she should have joined the police force like Sandy; as least Sandy got to carry a gun. Even Annie had been leading a more exciting life, defending Jack from a murder charge. And all Bolivia was getting was a reputation for putting humor in her columns. And that was only because she could rarely take her subject matter seriously.

She should quit. She had heard of other journalists who had lit off for the foreign country of their choice and gotten on as stringers for one of the wire services. She could sell her cycle. She had a little money in the bank. Well, actually very little, but she would only need airfare. Beirut. She would like to go to Beirut. For years she'd been dying to. And it wasn't all over there yet. Every time she thought it was, that she had finally missed out, something else would flare up.

She pictured herself living in one of those hotels that had been bombed so many times the only views weren't out of the windows. She pictured herself in the bar with the rest of the foreign correspondents, trading stories, rushing to file their news on the one telex available, sharing rides to whatever fighting was currently going on. And one thing was certain, it couldn't be any hotter there than it was in Miami. It might even be cooler.

She was in the middle of picturing herself being stopped by the Shiite militia when she realized that she had walked into the encampment. She brought her mind back to the present and looked around, only to find she was the one being looked at.

There were three men barbecuing something over a camp fire. All three were eyeing her with interest. Off to the right were two more men, sitting cross-legged on the ground and playing cards. They were all dressed in a motley assortment of army uniforms, some in camouflage, some not, some in T-shirts, a couple of them bare-chested. She counted five pup tents and one L.L. Bean Trail Dome model, the only one in bright orange.

There was dead silence at her arrival, except for the sounds of a radio turned low. At least they didn't seem to expect her.

"Good morning," said Bolivia, trying a smile. After all, she was alone in the middle of nowhere with five men who might or might not be crazy.

"You want something?" one of the men by the camp fire asked her.

Bolivia took the press card out of her shirt pocket and held it up. "I'm Smith from the *Times*. I'd like to interview you."

"No interviews," said one of the card players.

"I thought I could tell your side of the story," she said, trying it out.

That drew a response from the men at the camp fire.

"*What* story?" one of them wanted to know.

"There have been complaints about you. I figure you might want to justify your being here before the police check you out."

"We're not breaking any laws," said another of the men.

"You're scaring your good neighbors to the north," said Bolivia.

There were some grunts and a few laughs at that. "We're not bothering no one," said one of the guys, throwing down his cards in disgust.

"My newspaper has received several complaints, and I just talked to one of the women involved. She was personally concerned about your welfare, but she said that some of her neighbors are worried about their children."

"Get lost, lady."

Bolivia folded her arms across her chest. "Look, I'm going to write my story, with or without your help. Now, it can either be a story from your point of view, or it can be some negative publicity you might not want. It's up to you."

"We just want to be left alone." This from a guy who didn't look old enough to have been in Vietnam. Of course, Sandy didn't look old enough to be on the police force, either.

"Perhaps you could appoint one of you as spokesperson," said Bolivia, wondering what had ever induced her to come here in the first place. She would take police corruption over mosquito bites any day.

The guys at the camp fire went into a huddle; then one of them called over to one of the cardplayers, "Hey, Moose, you better go get Tooley. Tell him we've got a live one here."

*I'm* the live one? Bolivia felt like asking, but since she was outnumbered, she desisted.

As the messenger took off into the jungle, Bolivia took her camera out of her case.

"No pictures," yelled someone, and it sounded threatening enough that she put the camera back in the case.

"How about a picture of just the camp fire and tents?" she asked.

"No pictures!"

Bolivia decided to wait. Maybe this Tooley would be more amenable.

She had no sooner thought that when a crashing sound was heard, and then the mangroves parted and a man in a wheelchair came charging out of the jungle. The wheelchair had a rifle rack attached to the back of the seat, several bumper stickers pasted to it and a Red Sox pennant on a stick fastened to one of the arms. Over the wheels hung blue panniers. The man, so large he dwarfed the wheelchair, was wearing fatigue pants, a black tank top with a skull and crossbones on it, and he had a rifle across his lap. The most astonishing thing about him, though, was his hair. It was probably a more subdued color in the shade, but in the clearing it seemed to pick up all of the sunlight so that it looked as though it were on fire. Thick red waves of hair hung to well below his shoulders, and half his face was masked by a bushy mustache and beard. What wasn't covered by hair was a nose that looked as though it had been broken once or twice.

The red giant spoke. "What the hell are *you* doing here?"

Bolivia was very glad she was looking down at him. "That's what I was about to ask *you*."

She saw a flash of green from beneath his thick red brows. "You're trespassing, lady."

If there was anything Bolivia hated, it was being called *lady*. The last thing she ever aspired to be was a lady.

"This is public property," she countered.

The man wheeled up to within a few feet of her. She tried to outstare him but found herself backing off first. She pretended to be inspecting an insect that had landed on her arm.

"What do you think you're on, some kind of safari?" asked the man, sounding amused.

So she was wearing her Banana Republic clothes, so what? Wasn't that what all foreign correspondents wore? "I'm on an assignment," said Bolivia. "I'm with the *Miami Times*?"

His mouth turned up a little. "Am I supposed to drop dead at that news?"

"*You're* the news," said Bolivia.

"Says who?"

"Says your neighbors to the north. The property owners."

The man turned around and looked at the others. "You guys been fooling around out there?"

"No way, Tooley," said one of the men, and the others nodded.

"So what's the big complaint?" Tooley asked her.

"I think they're concerned about their teenage daughters," said Bolivia, and Tooley, gave a bark of laughter.

"We don't go after teenagers," he said.

"And drugs. They're concerned about drugs."

"Contrary to popular belief, lady, we don't do drugs. Not in any form."

Bolivia heard someone whisper to Tooley and caught the word *cat*.

"Get serious," said Tooley.

"What was that about a cat?" asked Bolivia.

"We didn't kill it," said Tooley. "It was hit by a car. We buried it, though."

"No one's accusing you of killing pets," said Bolivia.

Tooley lowered his head for a moment, and when he looked back up he was smiling and had a reasonable look on his face. She didn't trust it for a moment.

"Can I see some ID?" he asked her.

Bolivia took out her press card and held it out to him.

"Bolivia?" he said, reading off the card. "That's not a name, that's a country."

"I suppose *Tooley's* a name?"

"The name's Jim O'Toole," he said, "Tooley to my friends."

"Well, Mr. O'Toole," said Bolivia, "could I ask how you sustain yourselves out here?"

# Betrayed

She heard some sniggering from the men, which Tooley put an end to by saying, "She's talking about food, you illiterates."

Tooley grinned at her. "Well, you see, we wait for house pets to get run over, and then we barbecue them. Want to join us for lunch? It's just a cocker spaniel, but there's plenty to go around."

Bolivia grinned back at him. "Is that how you want to be quoted?"

"Who said I wanted to be quoted?"

"I thought I was interviewing you."

"You thought wrong," said Tooley, starting to turn his wheelchair around.

"Wait a minute," said Bolivia.

He looked back at her.

"Are you a paraplegic?"

This time his grin was mocking. "Nah, I'm just kinky. What do you think, this is my transportation of choice?"

"Do you want to talk about it?"

"Do I look like I want to talk about it?"

"Look, Tooley, you can either cooperate, in which case I'll put your point of view in the story, or you can be uncooperative, in which case I'll make sure every tourist coming to South Florida takes a side trip in here to get a look at you. Now, which is it going to be?"

Tooley picked up the rifle from his lap and pointed it at her. "You talk pretty brave, lady. What would happen if there was no one to write your story?"

"It's not loaded," said Bolivia.

Tooley rectified that in about two seconds.

"Go ahead, shoot," she said. "Then you'll really get some publicity."

Tooley unloaded the rifle and set it in the rack before exposing a full set of white teeth. "Care to join us for lunch, Bolivia?"

"I'd love to," she said, hoping it wasn't a house pet she was about to eat. Not that she might not have to eat worse in some warring Third World country, but this was Florida, after all.

They were seated on the ground a few feet from the heat of the camp fire, all except Tooley, who had distanced himself from them by moving his wheelchair slightly out of their circle. Bolivia felt him watching her as she ate. She didn't know exactly what it was she was eating; she had a feeling it was rabbit, mostly because it didn't taste like anything she'd ever had, and she had never had rabbit. She didn't like the idea of eating a bunny, but it was better than thinking she was eating a kitten or even a puppy.

With the meat, which had been put on sticks for ease of eating, there were also several orders of fries from McDonald's. A man she hadn't seen before had arrived shortly before they began eating, the familiar bags emblazoned with golden arches in his arms.

"I see you rough it," Bolivia had said to Tooley.

He laughed. "We don't live off the land, if that's what you mean."

"Where do you get the money?"

Tooley had raised his brows at this. "Do you always ask rude questions when people invite you to eat with them?"

"I was asking strictly as a reporter," said Bolivia.

"Right," agreed Tooley.

"I couldn't help wondering, that's all."

"Want to tell her how we get the money, guys?" Tooley asked the men.

"You mean besides mugging?" asked one of them.

"And robbing those nice ranch houses?" another chimed in.

"Forget it, I don't want to know," said Bolivia.

"And of course," said Tooley, his eyes gleaming, "I can always pick up a few bucks begging in my wheelchair. I've got this sign I wear around my neck that says 'Vietnam vet, I don't get any government benefits.'"

"That one I believe," said Bolivia, hoping to get a rise out of him, but he just laughed.

"If you want to know the truth," he said, "but this has to be off-the-record..." He waited for Bolivia's nod, and then said, "We take turns getting jobs when we need some money. Construction work, picking oranges, whatever's available. And I do happen to get disability checks from the government. We pool our money and make out okay."

There hadn't been any talk since then, and Bolivia had decided to finish eating before trying to interview them. They might be friendlier on a full stomach.

When some of the guys started lighting up cigarettes, Bolivia asked Tooley if it was okay to ask a few questions.

"Be my guest," he offered.

"What's your reason for being here?" she asked them in general.

"We like it here," said one of the men, and the others nodded in agreement.

"How did you know you'd like it to begin with?" she asked.

There were some looks exchanged, and then the youngest looking one said, "It's like it was in Nam."

"You *liked* Nam?" asked Bolivia.

"Life had some purpose to it there," she heard from one of them.

"Basically, it's the same old story," said Tooley. "We couldn't readjust to society when we got back. Most of us have broken marriages, most of us have been in group therapy, most of us were so traumatized by the war that we can no longer hold regular jobs."

That sounded a little too pat to Bolivia. Too much like everything she'd ever read about Vietnam vets. "You don't sound so traumatized," she told Tooley.

"Hey, you should see me when there's a full moon," he said, then grinned at her.

"You seem intelligent and articulate," she told him. "I don't see why you can't get a regular job."

"Pure prejudice," said Tooley.

"What?"

"You heard me. If we were a group of hippies, you wouldn't say that. If we were a group of hippies and had formed a commune to avoid the rat race of the eighties, you'd think we were wonderful. But because we fought in the war, we're suspect."

"You're mistaking me for someone else," said Bolivia. "Hippies were before my time."

"We're heroes," said one of the men. "Didn't you see *Platoon*?"

"I also saw *Rambo*," said Bolivia, and got a laugh from the men.

"Look, we like it here," said Tooley. "The climate's good, the rent can't be beat, and there aren't any utility bills. I mean, who else do you know who lives in Fort Lauderdale and can say that?"

"Don't you have any ambition?" she asked him. She couldn't understand people who had no ambition.

"I don't," said Tooley. "You guys have any?" he asked the men.

"Not me," they all agreed.

"What's your ambition, Bolivia?" asked Tooley. "To bother people who don't want to talk to you?"

She guessed that was as good a description of her job as any. "I like covering the news."

"And we're news?" asked one of the guys.

"Not yet," said Bolivia. "But you will be after I've written my column."

"Oh, a columnist," said one of them, dismissing her.

"You write a gossip column or what?" asked another.

"I'm an investigative reporter," said Bolivia. "Usually I write about corruption of some kind."

"Then what are you doing here?" asked Tooley. "What happened, was it a slow week?"

"Actually, it was," she said.

"Well, let's see if we can make up something interesting for you," said Tooley. "How about this. We were brainwashed by the Viet Cong, and we're building our own little communist society in the middle of Florida."

"Try again," said Bolivia.

"I got it," said one of the guys. "You could say we're at a summer camp for veterans. That'd be good publicity. Maybe we could get some more guys."

"Yeah, and we could charge for it," said another.

"Let's not make it sound too good," said Tooley, "or we'll have every redneck within a hundred miles wanting to play war games with us."

"You play war games?" asked Bolivia.

"Oh, hell, yes!" said Tooley. "Tell her about our games, men."

"Let's see," said one. "There's five card stud."

"And there's kick the can," said another. "You've never played kick the can until you've played it here. I don't think we've found a can yet."

"Bobby Joe and I play chess," said another.

"What's your game?" Bolivia asked Tooley.

He grinned at her. "You don't want to know."

"If I didn't want to know, I wouldn't ask."

He cocked his head in the direction of the orange tent. "You see that tent over there?"

"I see it."

"Come on over and I'll show you my game."

"No thanks," said Bolivia.

"Did you ever see the movie *Coming Home*?"

"I saw it."

He grinned. "You know what the biggest advantage is to being in a wheelchair?"

"If you're going to say sex . . ."

The men were suddenly convulsed with laughter, but Tooley just kept grinning. "You see one of the great movies of all time, and the only thing that makes an impression on you is the sex, am I right? Forget the layers of meaning, forget the theme, discount entirely the fact that it's a metaphor for life, just zero in on the fact that a guy in a wheelchair might not be able to—"

"I don't want to hear this," said Bolivia, very sorry she had said what she had. This was one more time when her big mouth was likely to get her in trouble.

"Anyway," said Tooley, "the biggest advantage to being in a wheelchair is going to the head of the line at the movies and always getting an aisle seat."

"How do you get to a theater?" Bolivia asked him.

Tooley nodded. "That's the problem."

"You want some coffee, ma'am?" one of the guys asked her.

# Betrayed

"Sure, thanks," said Bolivia. The damnedest thing was, she was enjoying herself. The day was still hot, the food had been lousy, but she was having the best time she'd had in ages. "Could I get a picture of you guys?" she asked.

"No pictures," said Tooley.

"Why not?"

"I know you journalists have trouble believing this, Bolivia, but not everyone wants to see his picture in the paper. No pictures. An invitation to lunch does not include a photo opportunity."

"It was really for me," said Bolivia. "I just write a column. I don't get to have pictures accompanying it."

"I'll tell you what," said Tooley. "Since all you want is a souvenir of your visit with us, you can sit on my lap, and Moose will take a picture of us together."

"That's not what I had in mind," said Bolivia.

"Take it or leave it," said Tooley.

Bolivia left it.

She was handed a mug of coffee, and even offered sugar. She turned down the sugar and took a sip of the coffee. It was terrible, almost as bad as the coffee she made.

"Is there anything you'd like me to say about you?" she asked them. However, she wasn't sure at this point whether she'd even use the information. It wasn't turning out to be interesting enough for a column.

Tooley actually stopped grinning long enough to place a thoughtful expression on his face. "Just say we don't intend to bother anyone, and we would just as soon no one bothered us. We're here to live a quiet life of contemplation, rather like monks."

"Monks don't carry rifles," said Bolivia, not believing a word he said.

"It's strictly for hunting," said Tooley, "and not against the law."

"What do you hunt?"

"Quail, rabbits, that's about it. And not much of that, if you want to know the truth. We just feel safer having them, that's all. You'd understand if you'd ever been in a war."

Bolivia must have given something away with her expression, because Tooley immediately said, "What was that look for? You been to war?"

"Not yet," said Bolivia.

"Meaning?"

"Meaning I'd like to, but I never get sent. Every time there's a war, they send a man."

"I think we have ourselves a frustrated foreign correspondent," Tooley said to the men. "Shall we play some war games for her and make her happy?"

"Ah, hell, Tooley, that means we'd have to clean our rifles," said one of the men.

"The noise just gives me a headache," said another.

Tooley looked at Bolivia and shrugged. "Well, I tried."

As though on cue the men all got up and started heading for the pup tents. Only Tooley stayed in place.

"Where are they going?" Bolivia asked him.

"It's siesta time," said Tooley. "Any civilized person knows you don't sit out in the midday sun."

"Well, I guess I'd better be going," said Bolivia, standing up and brushing off the seat of her pants.

"You're welcome to stay," said Tooley. "My tent sleeps two."

"No, thank you."

"You could make a poor old vet happy."

"You look happy enough to me," said Bolivia, seeing his grin once again.

"I could be happier."

"We could all be happier," said Bolivia.

"You're a tough woman, lady."

"I enjoyed lunch," said Bolivia.

"I can guarantee you'd like the siesta even more."

There was something about this kind of talk coming from a man in a wheelchair that failed to be scary. "I think you see too many movies," she said.

His eyes took on a more serious look as he said, "Sometimes you're forced to live vicariously."

For a moment she was half tempted to say, *Get rid of your men, Tooley, and you've got yourself a deal.* The next moment she was saying, "I think it's time for me to hit the road."

She could have sworn, from his final grin at her, that he'd known exactly what she was thinking.

He wheeled over with her to where the path began. "Can you find your way out?" he asked her.

"No problem," said Bolivia.

"I can send one of the guys with you if you want."

"If I can find my way in, I can find my way out."

"Be like that."

She softened for a moment and held out her hand. "It's been a pleasure meeting you, Jim O'Toole."

"Likewise, Bolivia," he said, grasping her hand firmly and applying a little pressure. And then he was wheeling around in his chair and heading for his tent.

Bolivia was a few yards down the path when she got the idea to sneak back and take a picture of the camp. Even if she didn't use it in the paper, she'd like to have it to show Annie and Sandy. And to keep as a memento.

She walked back quietly, taking care not to make a sound. When she was almost to the clearing she heard laughter and ducked behind a tree. She moved forward, keeping out of sight, until, when she peered around the last tree, she saw the men gathered around Tooley. They must have been kidding him, and it made a great picture, so she took out her Nikon and took a couple of shots.

She didn't even feel like a sneak. It was what reporters did, wasn't it.

Sneak was the name of the game.

## Chapter 3

The headwaiter gave them a second look, and then a third. Okay, so they were a strange looking threesome, but he must have seen stranger in Miami, with all the oddly assorted tourists it attracted. Bolivia had a tendency to blame everything from crime to the weather on the tourists. Luckily, her occupation wasn't one that had to cater to them.

Anne, having just come from work, was looking like a fashion model in cream linen and black silk, her curly blond hair kept under control by a straw hat pulled low. She could actually walk gracefully in her high heels, which was something Bolivia gave her credit for. Bolivia couldn't walk unless her feet were firmly planted on the ground. She was wearing her usual, which meant khaki pants and khaki shirt, and a bola with a turquoise stone around her neck. The bola was her one concession to dressing up for the occasion of a meal in a good restaurant. Sandy, she guessed, was getting most of the attention. But Sandy was required by her job to have her gun on her at all times, and it just wasn't that easy to conceal a gun beneath a Hawaiian shirt hanging outside her shorts. What was working in her favor was that she looked young enough, especially in the high-top sneakers, that the gun could conceivably be a toy.

"I want something very strong and very cold," said Bolivia as soon as they were seated. She took note of the fact that the waiter had placed them behind a rather prominent potted palm.

"You're going to need it," murmured Sandy.

"What's that supposed to mean?"

Sandy didn't answer, just glanced over at Anne, who rather rapidly picked up the menu and began studying it.

Bolivia sensed a conspiracy. "What don't I know?" she asked.

"Loved your column today," said Anne, looking up from her menu long enough to give Bolivia a big smile. Well, that smile might work on every man who came into contact with her, but it wasn't going to work on Bolivia. Since when did Annie have to turn the charm on for *her* benefit?

The waiter came by for their drink order, and Bolivia decided to make it a double. Just as insurance.

"You made them sound adventurous and wonderful," said Sandy. "The guys in the jungle camp."

"In a way, they were," said Bolivia, still eyeing Annie with distrust.

"I wouldn't have thought a bunch of Vietnam vets would appeal to you," said Anne.

"I'm sure we aren't here to discuss my column," said Bolivia.

"We're here to have dinner," said Anne. "The conversation is just the icing on the cake."

"And speaking of cakes..." said Sandy.

"Shut up!" Anne warned her.

"I didn't say a word," said Sandy.

"It's not my birthday," said Bolivia. "And it's not one of your birthdays, either. So I have to assume the cake in question is a wedding cake."

"Don't look at me," said Anne. "I wasn't the one who mentioned a cake."

Sandy was sliding down in her chair and practically disappearing under the table.

"What is this?" asked Bolivia. "We going to be discussing weddings from now on, is that it? Where's your copy of *Modern Bride*, Annie? Are you going to drag that out next? Correct me if I'm wrong, but I thought we made fun of women like that. The kind who sit around beauty parlors and talk about their china patterns."

Damned if Annie didn't turn pink.

"I don't believe it," said Bolivia. "Don't tell me you actually have a china pattern. Excuse me while I go to the ladies' room and barf."

"No, of course I don't have a china pattern," said Anne. "Why would I have a china pattern? I don't even cook."

"You getting your hope chest set up, is that it?" Bolivia could hear the sarcasm in her own voice but didn't give a damn. The reason they were such good friends was because they *didn't* discuss things like that. Now, overnight, things were changing. Hell, if she wanted to discuss weddings, all she had to do was phone her mother.

"Look, if my having a wedding is going to ruin our friendship, I'll forget about it," said Anne, sounding very businesslike.

"Nothing's going to ruin our friendship," said Sandy.

"If we could just not talk about it all the time," said Bolivia.

"You sound like Jack," said Anne.

"Wait a minute," said Bolivia. "I thought it was Jack who wanted a wedding."

"At first. But now it's my mother who's promoting a big one."

"Didn't your mother have a wedding?"

"I only have one thing to say about it, and then we can talk about something else for the rest of the evening," said Anne.

"Okay, what is it?" asked Bolivia.

Anne reached into her handbag. "I just want you to approve something, that's all." She drew out a picture and passed it first to Sandy.

Sandy's scowl went into place. "I'm going to look like a twelve-year-old in that," she grumbled, passing it on to Bolivia.

"No, you're not," said Anne.

"Sure she is," said Bolivia. "Sandy looks twelve in everything." Then she looked down at the picture. It showed a willowy blond model wearing a pink dress that reached her ankles with a large bow in the back. It was the bow that got to her. She had refused anything with bows on it as a child, and she wasn't going to change her mind about them now. "No way," she said, handing the picture back to Anne.

"That's going to make me look like a flower girl," said Sandy. "I can put a ribbon in my hair and be a dark Alice in Wonderland."

Annie gave them both an exasperated look, ripped the picture into pieces and put the pieces in the unused ashtray. "Okay, guys, you want to tell me your ideas of what a bridesmaid should look like?"

"What kind of shoes would we have to wear?" asked Bolivia.

"Are you asking me to choose between your hiking boots and your running shoes?" Anne asked her.

"I'm not wearing heels," said Bolivia.

"I'm not wearing flats," said Sandy. "Not if I'm going to be standing next to Bolivia."

"Could you take the bow off?" asked Bolivia.

"Yes, we can take the bow off," said Anne, sounding very much as though she were humoring little children. "What about you, Sandy? Any alterations you want?"

"I'm going to look so juvenile in those short, puffed sleeves," said Sandy.

"That thing with the flowers on it is going to look stupid on my short hair," said Bolivia. "I'm going to look like a guy in drag."

Anne studied them both for a minute. "Is there *anything* you like about it?"

"Well," said Sandy.

"Uh," said Bolivia.

"All right, I'll try again," said Anne. "Where are our drinks? I could really use mine."


"The one in the wheelchair," said Bolivia, pointing out Tooley to them.

Anne bent over the photograph. "Not bad. He looks like a musician." Anne had been attracted to musicians before Jack came along.

"He looks dangerous to me, all that dark hair," said Sandy. "He looks exactly like one-third of the prison population."

"It's red," said Bolivia. "He'd look better in a color photograph. It's that real orangy color like they use for life jackets."

"Is there some reason for showing us this?" asked Anne. "I already saw it in the paper today."

"The one in the paper wasn't as clear," said Bolivia, looking down at Tooley's face and smiling at the memory.

"Did you see that?" asked Sandy. "She's smiling at the guy."

"I saw it," said Anne. "Not Bolivia's usual behavior, I agree.

"I'm not smiling at him," said Bolivia. "I'm smiling at the memory of our conversation that's all. He's pretty funny."

"Oh, yes," said Sandy. "Must be a bundle of laughs living in the jungle in a wheelchair."

"Is he paraplegic?" asked Anne.

"I don't know. I assume so," said Bolivia.

"Could be an amputee," said Sandy. "Or maybe he just got his legs shattered."

"He's got to be a weirdo, living in the middle of the jungle like that," said Anne.

"At least slightly crazed," said Sandy.

"Forget it," said Bolivia, grabbing the picture off the table and putting it back in her pocket.

"She's sulking now," said Anne.

"I noticed," said Sandy.

"It's not like our Bolivia to sulk." Anne was being her amusing self, and Bolivia felt like kicking her.

"I think she's interested in him," said Sandy.

"Not possible," said Anne. "Bolivia's only interest in men is competitive."

Sandy laughed. "Bolivia's only interest in *any*thing is competitive."

"Too true," said Anne.

"You've got two choices," said Bolivia. "You can shut up and I'll stay or you can continue to harangue me and I'll go."

"Harangue?" asked Anne. "The investigative reporter with the biggest mouth in Miami, and you're accusing us of haranguing?"

"Just keep it up, Annie," warned Bolivia.

"It all makes sense now," said Sandy, acting as though she had suddenly solved a murder case.

"Not to me," said Anne.

"Yes," said Sandy. "Listen to this. Bolivia's interested in him because he's safe."

"I thought you said he looked like a criminal?"

"But as a man he's safe," said Sandy.

"Obviously, you didn't see *Coming Home*," said Anne.

"I saw it," said Sandy. "We all rented it together, if you recall. I'm not talking about sexually, though. I'm talking about the fact that he's dropped out of society. It stands to reason he doesn't date."

"I've had enough of this," said Bolivia, pushing back her chair and standing up.

"We haven't even had dessert yet," said Anne.

"I'm not going to sit here and be bad-mouthed by my two best friends any longer."

"Was he sexy?" asked Anne.

Bolivia relaxed a little. "Extremely."

"That means he fought with her," said Sandy. "Ever since the fourth grade, Bolivia has always gone for guys who fight with her."

"That's not true," said Bolivia, sitting back down.

"Was it mutual?" asked Anne.

"Of course it was mutual," said Bolivia. "We were mutually antagonistic from the word go."

Sandy rolled her eyes. "Well, that's Bolivia's idea of romance, all right."

"I love fighting with men," said Bolivia. "There's a certain energy to it."

"Especially if you wind up in bed," said Sandy.

"Did you?" asked Anne.

"What are you? Crazy?" asked Bolivia. "We weren't exactly alone."

"Are you going to see him again?" asked Sandy.

"I'm afraid not," said Bolivia.

"Why not?" asked Anne. "What's stopping you from visiting him again?"

"I'm not going chasing after some guy," said Bolivia. "Anyway, I'm not interested."

"Oh, right," said Sandy. "She's just carrying his picture around in her pocket, but she's not interested."

"I thought maybe you hadn't seen it in the paper," said Bolivia.

"You kill us if we don't read your column," said Anne.

"If they'd ever give me an overseas assignment, I'd probably meet lots of men like him," said Bolivia.

"It wouldn't work out, anyway," said Sandy. "There's no way he could get his wheelchair on your motorcycle."

"There's no way I could get *him* on my motorcycle," said Bolivia. "I haven't seen him standing up, of course, but he looked like a giant."

Over dessert they started their usual argument over which movie they were going to see. Sandy favored movies with romance in them, which Bolivia hated. She preferred movies that didn't even have women in them. Anne liked science fiction, particularly if the film had great special effects. Sandy didn't enjoy science fiction. They all like movies about cops, but there wasn't one currently playing. They finally compromised on a suspense film, but Bolivia was certain there was going to be a romance in it somewhere. She was right about that and fell asleep right around when the second kiss occurred. When she heard afterward that the second kiss had very quickly evolved into a murder, she could have kicked herself for not staying awake. On the other hand, it had been very nice to get some sleep in an air-conditioned place for a change.

"What're you guys doing this weekend," Bolivia asked as they got out of the movie theater.

"Jack and I—" Anne started to say.

"I don't even want to hear it," said Bolivia. "You're probably going to check out silverware or something."

"Give it a rest, Bolivia," said Anne. "All I was going to say was that we were driving down to the Keys. You're welcome to come along if you want."

"Thanks, but I think I'll give it a miss," said Bolivia. The last thing she felt like doing was spending the weekend with a couple in love. Anyway, they deserved some privacy; Jack was probably getting tired of having Bolivia and Sandy around half the time.

"What about you?" Bolivia asked Sandy.

"I have to work this weekend. A stakeout of a suspected crack house."

"That sounds fun," said Bolivia, meaning it.

"Not in the back of a van without air-conditioning."

"Sounds just like my room," said Bolivia.

She ended up not doing much of anything all weekend, except swimming in the warm ocean and eating too much junk food. The only thing of any consequence she did was buy a hammock and string it across her small terrace. Visiting the jungle camp had given her the idea. Her body covered with insect repellant, she slept outside both Saturday and Sunday nights. It was only slightly cooler than sleeping indoors, but it made her feel adventurous.

*It was a typical night in Beirut. Outside the hotel, the Syrians and the Christians were shelling their respective areas of the city; inside, the journalists were crowded into the bar. The booze was flowing as freely as the war stories when Bolivia made her entrance.*

*She was looking good: slim and dark, a little battle weary, slightly jaded. The aviator sunglasses, worn night and day, added just the right touch. She had heard that some of the stringers had started to refer to her as the Snake. The name alluded to the fact that she could slink into dangerous circumstances unobserved and sneak back out with an exclusive. She liked the appellation and was thinking of incorporating it into her byline.*

*A hush came over the bar at her arrival. Then whispers started up, and the word "snake" could be heard along the length of the bar. As lowly stringers parted to give her room, Bolivia slouched over to where the cream of the European reporters were holding forth. The bartender scuttled down to her end of the bar, and she said, "Bombay gin on the rocks, Khalid. Better make it a double."*

*Ferguson, the Tribune bureau chief, placed a comradely arm around her shoulders. "The word is you're onto something, Smith," he said, the slightest trace of awe in his voice.*

*"Maybe," said Bolivia, downing the gin and nodding to the bartender for another.*

*"We hear it has to do with the hostages."*

# Betrayed 51

*She gave an almost imperceptible nod and was instantly surrounded. They'd try to interrogate her, but she was up to it. There was no way they were wily enough to get the information out of her that was sure to lead to the journalistic coup of her career.*

*There was the sound of an explosion behind her, and she waited a second or two before casually glancing around. The lobby of the hotel had taken a direct hit, and she saw that several of the newer stringers had hit the floor. The old timers, like herself, barely paused in their drinking.*

*As the premier group of reporters began to drift toward the exit, one of the stringers grabbed hold of Bolivia's arm.*

*"Where are we going?" he asked, his eyes looking frantic. "Are we going to the bomb shelter?"*

*A few minutes later they were all crowded onto the balcony of her room, watching the distant—and not so distant—shelling. It was rather like watching the fireworks display on the Fourth of July on Miami Beach. The only thing missing was the ocean.*

The ringing of the phone on her desk brought Bolivia abruptly back to reality.

"Is this Bolivia Smith?" a woman asked her.

"It is," said the Snake.

"It's about your column last Friday."

Bolivia had a feeling it was one of the women from the neighborhood in Fort Lauderdale complaining about what she'd written.

"What about it?" Bolivia asked.

"Well, actually, it's about the picture."

"What about the picture?"

"You're going to think I'm crazy..." The woman's voice trailed off in uncertainty.

So Tooley had appealed to someone else, too. Well, Bolivia wasn't going to introduce her, if that was what she wanted.

"Don't worry about it, I'm feeling a little crazy myself this morning," Bolivia told her.

"Well, the thing is . . . one of the men in the picture is my husband."

"The one with the red hair?"

"The picture's in black-and-white."

"Yeah, right," said Bolivia. "The one in the wheelchair?"

"No, the man standing to his left. The good looking one with the dark hair."

"Hold it, let me get the picture," said Bolivia, opening her desk drawer and taking out a copy. That was her idea of good looking? Bolivia thought the man looked perfectly ordinary next to Tooley. But then, maybe Tooley wasn't everyone's type.

"Okay, I see him," said Bolivia.

"His name is Eldon," said the woman. "Eldon Waring. I'm Jenny Waring."

"I didn't meet him," said Bolivia. "I had lunch with them, but I wasn't introduced."

"He disappeared," said Jenny Waring, "a couple of months ago. Didn't take anything. Just walked out of the house, said he was going to the liquor store, and never came back."

"I'm sorry," said Bolivia. "I would guess most of them have a story like that to tell. Not being able to readjust to civilian life and all that."

"You don't understand," said Jenny. "What you say in your article, about all of them being Vietnam vets..."

"Right," said Bolivia.

"Eldon was never in Vietnam. Eldon was never even in the army. Or any other branch of the military."

"It's probably a case of mistaken identity," said Bolivia.

"I think I know my own husband when I see him."

"Well, the picture isn't all that clear. He could be a lot of guys."

Jenny started crying.

"Hey, I'm sorry," said Bolivia.

"I think you're wrong," said Jenny, her voice catching. "My husband disappeared, and then I see his picture in the paper and now you're saying I don't even recognize my own husband."

"What can I tell you?" said Bolivia. "They were all Vietnam vets."

"Eldon wasn't old enough to go to Vietnam. He's only thirty."

"Look, if I blew up the picture, I'm sure you would realize you'd made a mistake. He isn't even that clear in the picture. I think he was moving."

"Would you?" asked Jenny.

"Would I what?"

"Would you blow up the picture for me?"

"Would that satisfy you?"

"Yes, please. Could I come down there?"

"I'm rather busy right now—"

"Please? I'll just take a look at it, and then I'll go, okay? I mean, the police wouldn't take it seriously, and I was beginning to doubt myself. I'd feel so much better if I was sure it was Eldon."

"Oh, why not," said Bolivia. "Come on down."

Jenny turned out to be an extremely pretty little blonde, exactly the sort of woman Bolivia had always thought men went for. So why had her husband walked out?

She handed Jenny the 8 × 10 blowup of the section of the picture showing the man to Tooley's left.

"Yes, that's Eldon," said Jenny, tears threatening the corners of her eyes.

"Are you sure?" asked Bolivia.

"Would you know your husband if you saw a picture of him in the newspaper?" asked Jenny.

"I don't have a husband," said Bolivia.

"Do you have a boss?"

"Yes."

"Would you know him?"

"Yes, I would," said Bolivia.

Jenny opened up her white handbag and brought out a wedding picture, handing it over to Bolivia. The picture immediately depressed Bolivia, as it had bridesmaids in the background, and they were wearing, curiously enough, pink.

Bolivia recognized Eldon right away, though. She hadn't from her own picture, but she did from this. He was the one she had thought looked so young. Too young to have served in Vietnam.

"I remember him," said Bolivia.

Jenny sighed. "Thank God someone finally believes me."

"It seems strange he'd go to live with a bunch of veterans," mused Bolivia.

"Everything's been strange," said Jenny. "I mean, I could understand if he walked out after a fight, but everything was fine. We'd only just moved here, too. I mean, why up and move me away from my family and friends if he was planning on leaving me?"

"Stranger things happen."

"I guess," said Jenny, "but Eldon was never that imaginative. He was just so nice and ordinary. Good looking, but just an every day kind of person. Which is why he appealed to me."

"Well, look," said Bolivia, "why don't I tell you how to get there? It sounds as though you two need to talk."

"Oh, no," said Jenny, all traces of tears disappearing. "I'm not going to go chasing after him. If he wants to talk to me, he can just cut out this nonsense and come home. I'm just glad to know he's all right. I was afraid he might've been hit by a car or dropped dead somewhere."

"You sure?" asked Bolivia, thinking she wouldn't mind a second trip into the jungle herself. "I'll go along with you, if you want."

Jenny shook her head. "I never chased after a guy in my life, and I'm not about to start now."

Bolivia wondered if her going back to the camp would constitute her chasing after Tooley. Probably, but, unlike Jenny, she wasn't above chasing a man on occasion.

Bolivia breezed into her boss's office and waited for him to get off the phone. Once she was sitting there listening in, he didn't feel inclined to prolong the conversation and soon hung up. She had a feeling it hadn't been work-related.

"What's up?" Henry asked her.

"That column I did last week—"

"Very favorable response," he said. "I personally thought it was one of your better columns."

"I thought it was kind of boring," said Bolivia.

"You don't have to always be exposing things in order to be interesting," said Henry. "It had a certain poignancy..."

Bolivia grimaced. Poignancy wasn't something she wanted to be known for. Hard-hitting facts, that was more her speed. "I was wondering if you'd be interested in a follow-up?" she asked.

"What'd you have in mind?"

Bolivia told him about Jenny. "I just thought human interest, you know? Disappearing husband, found because of a column in the *Times*. I guess it's a lousy idea."

"It has possibilities," said Henry. "Not your usual thing, though."

"No."

"But I like it. I mean, we're always exposing things. This time we were responsible for something nice happening. Unless something more interesting comes up before Friday."

"What I was thinking," said Bolivia, "is that it might be even better if I were to go back to the camp and confront the missing husband. Maybe get his side of the story, too. I personally would like to know why a guy who isn't even a veteran is living there with all those gung-ho types."

"Go for it," said Henry. "You know something, Bolivia? I can see you evolving into a completely different kind of reporter. Not human interest, exactly, but—"

"Go to hell, Henry."

"Excuse me?"

"You heard me. If you think I'm going to evolve into some kind of domesticated animal, you're wrong. I want Beirut, Henry. And if not Beirut, at least Managua."

Henry gave a long-suffering sigh. "Bolivia, Bolivia, when are you going to—"

Bolivia stalked out of his office.

## Chapter 4

The boat steamed into the wide river in the early evening. It was absolutely still. The air smelled cool, and the banks looked wild and barren, shadowed in purple. Fireflies were not yet awake, no fish broke the surface of the water, even the bullfrogs had not begun their nightly choir practice.

The sun and the moon blazed at each other, not palely apart, but each a fiery presence low in the sky, glowing, vivid, alive. The Amazon was no longer muddy water, but solid metal, oddly luminous. One side was silver, slightly tinged with mauve. The other was blinding gold hammered into a vast sheet.

Suddenly something happened that shattered the peace. Bolivia's Indian guide pointed to the water, and there, in its luminous depths, was a leaping, struggling mass of silver fish. It lurked like a cloud beneath the surface and stretched for many yards in a great circle. The guide threw the carcass of the boar they had had for *dinner into the midst of the commotion. In an instant it was gone, rent in pieces by the waiting shoal.*

*"Piranha," said the guide, spitting thoughtfully.*

*In the next instant the guide had tumbled overboard, and then Bolivia was all alone on the Amazon, miles from civilization, the feared headhunters somewhere ahead in the growing darkness.*

Bolivia pulled up to the curb and parked her motorcycle. She saw a curtain move in one of the houses, but she ignored it and crossed the street to take the path she had traversed before.

Maybe it wasn't a real jungle, but she was still excited. It seemed real. It seemed completely removed from civilization. It was at the opposite end of reality from I-95, with the traffic backed up for miles because of an overturned tractor-trailer. By squinting her eyes she could imagine dark forms lurking behind the trees and tracking her every move.

Then a real form, not so dark, jumped out onto the path in front of her and blocked her way. He didn't look familiar from her previous visit.

"What's your business here?" she was asked.

"I'm Smith of the *Times*," she said, but from the lack of recognition on his face, he didn't appear to be one of her fans.

"I asked you what your business was." The guy seemed deadly serious.

"I could ask you the same thing," said Bolivia, trying to lighten things up.

He wasn't amused.

"I want to see Tooley, okay?"

"What about?"

"None of your business."

The man aimed his M-16 into the air and fired off a shot.

"What are you? Crazy?" yelled Bolivia. "That's a sure way to get the cops in here, you know."

"Follow me," he said.

"I know my way."

"I said, follow me!"

The man walked so slowly that Bolivia felt like passing him on the left, but every time she tried, he blocked her path.

When they got to the clearing she saw Tooley wheeling up to meet her. Her guard with the rifle moved off, and, looking beyond Tooley, Bolivia thought there were more men present than had been there during her first visit.

Tooley was bare chested today, and thick, red hair covered his chest and forearms and crept out from under his arms.

"Hello again," said Tooley, very low-key. If she had expected pleasure at her unexpected visit, it didn't look as though she was going to get it.

"How's it going?" asked Bolivia.

Tooley didn't seem in the mood for small talk. "Is there some reason for your coming back?" he asked.

Obviously he hadn't been fantasizing about her the way she had about him. She felt somewhat foolish. "I was wondering if you saw my column about you," she said.

"Where'd you get the picture?" he asked, answering her question.

"Well..."

"I told you no pictures."

"People always say that, but—"

"I meant it," said Tooley. "We cooperated with you, against my better judgment, and you took advantage of us."

"Look, I'm a reporter."

"No wonder you people are so universally loathed."

"War correspondents aren't loathed," said Bolivia.

"How would you know?"

Bolivia dug into the dirt with the toe of one shoe. "Okay, Tooley, so you aren't glad to see me. I can take a hint."

"Obviously, you can't. You took a picture of us without our permission."

"I don't see what the big deal is—"

"You wouldn't!"

"As a matter of fact, I'm here because of the picture."

There was no reaction from Tooley.

Bolivia looked around and saw that all the men had gathered a few feet behind Tooley and were watching them. Not one face appeared friendly. She tried out a tentative smile on them, but no one responded. She quickly changed the smile into a scowl.

"A woman called me," said Bolivia, "when she saw the picture in the paper. She recognized her husband, who had disappeared."

Tooley looked down at the ground and shook his head in disgust.

"She was worried about him," said Bolivia.

"What's this got to do with me?"

"He was with you."

"Look, Bolivia, the truth of the matter is, we don't want you around here."

Last time he invited her into his tent, this time he wanted her gone. She couldn't figure him out. "I'm staying anyway," said Bolivia, "until I get a chance to talk to Eldon."

"Who?"

"Eldon Waring, the woman's husband."

"Never heard of him," said Tooley.

"Well, he was here, because I remember him."

Tooley turned around to the men. "Any of you guys Eldon Waring?"

No one spoke.

"There's your answer," said Tooley.

"That's no answer at all," said Bolivia, taking the picture out of her pocket. She held it out to Tooley, and when he didn't take it, she tossed it onto his lap.

He looked down at the picture. "When did you take it?"

"Right after I left," said Bolivia.

"What did you do, sneak back?"

She nodded.

"I knew I should've had someone escort you out. Damn nosy reporters!"

"I wasn't being nosy," said Bolivia, wondering why she felt the need to explain herself to him. "Anyway, I didn't intend it for the paper. They've never used one of my pictures before."

"They did this time."

Bolivia shrugged.

"What did you intend it for?"

"It was just . . . an impulse."

"Which one is he?" asked Tooley.

Bolivia took a step forward and leaned over to point out Eldon.

"That's Buddy," said Tooley.

"Whatever."

"He's not here anymore."

"I don't believe you," said Bolivia.

Tooley turned to the men. "Any of you guys know where Buddy took off to?"

The men shook their heads.

"I think he's hiding," said Bolivia.

"Be serious," said Tooley. "If you ran away from your wife and were hiding out here, and some reporter put a picture of you in the newspaper, would you stick around?"

"I don't have a wife" said Bolivia. "Or a husband, either."

"I could tell that, but that wasn't the question."

"I was hoping I could talk to him, tell him how worried his wife is," said Bolivia.

"What are you, a marriage counselor on the side?"

"I just thought it would make a good follow-up story."

"That sounds more like the truth."

"What did you mean when you said you could tell that?"

"What're you talking about?" asked Tooley.

"About my not being married."

"I can tell a married woman from an unmarried woman, that's all."

"How?"

"By your look of desperation," said Tooley, a sudden gleam in his eyes.

She felt like kicking him in the leg, only that wasn't a very nice thing to do to someone in a wheelchair. "Very funny," she said. "If I had a husband and he ran away, I'd say good riddance."

"Well, if that's all..." said Tooley, turning his wheelchair around and riding off.

"Wait a minute," said Bolivia, following after him.

# Betrayed

The men closed in to block her way, their rifles pointed at her.

"What are you going to do, shoot me?" asked Bolivia.

Dead silence.

"Tooley, I just want to ask you a few more questions."

"The interview is over," said Tooley, his back to her.

"This is important. The woman said her husband was never in Vietnam. He wasn't even in the army."

"So?"

"So what was he doing in a camp with a bunch of veterans?"

Tooley slowly wheeled around to face her. "We don't ask for credentials here."

"You just let anyone in?"

"Anyone with a need," said Tooley.

"You mean anyone running away?"

"Look," he said, "all I know about Buddy is that he showed up a couple of weeks ago and took off shortly after you were here."

"Before his picture was in the paper?"

"What day was it in?"

"Friday."

Tooley nodded. "I guess he doesn't like reporters."

"Did he tell anyone where he was going?"

Tooley spoke to one of the men for a moment. "He told Bobby Joe he was heading north. Said he couldn't take the heat."

"He could've been a criminal for all you know," said Bolivia.

"Escort her out," said Tooley, wheeling over to the orange tent.

"I'm not through yet," Bolivia started to say, but then a couple of guys with M-16s pointed at her started in her direction, and she turned around and headed down the path. She could hear them behind her all the way but didn't give them the satisfaction of turning around.

It wasn't until she got her motorcycle started that she looked back to see if they were still there, but they were gone.

"What'd you get?" asked Henry.

"Nothing." She was in such a foul mood that she even felt like kicking Henry. Not that she didn't often feel like kicking her boss.

"Nothing?"

*"Nada,"* said Bolivia. "Eldon Waring flew the coop, and nobody knows anything. Or so they claim."

"Oh, well, it wasn't your style anyway," said Henry. "Got any other ideas?"

"How about slum landlords who go away to Alaska for the summer and turn off the air-conditioning in the hotel."

"You talking about Arthur and Julie again?"

Bolivia nodded.

"Look, they might not be ethical, but what they do isn't illegal."

"Henry, do you know where I've been sleeping nights?"

"I don't figure that's any of my business, Bolivia."

"On my balcony. In a hammock. Five hundred bucks a month, and I have to sleep outdoors."

"Write about the Nicaraguans."

"Send me to Managua and I will."

"In the baseball stadium. They have the refugees camping out in the baseball stadium."

"At least they're not paying five hundred a month for the privilege," said Bolivia.

"Jenny? This is Bolivia Smith."

"Oh, hi," said Jenny.

"I went back out to the jungle camp today. Thought I might be able to get another story out of it."

"If you saw my husband, I'm not interested."

"That's the strange part," said Bolivia. "He wasn't there. He took off shortly after I was out there the first time."

"I'm not surprised," said Jenny.

"No one knew anything about him. They called him Buddy."

"His family calls him Buddy."

"The thing is, he's acting like he has something to hide. Something more than just his disappearing husband act."

"Not Eldon."

"I was wondering if he was in any kind of trouble at work." She was thinking along the lines of embezzlement but didn't like to come right out with it.

"They won't even talk to me where he worked. They don't even return my calls."

"Want me to call them?"

"No. I'm so angry at him I could scream. Leaves me with all the bills and just takes off."

"Maybe you ought to contact the police again. They ought to be able to find him for you."

"They could hardly wait to get rid of me."

"Look, I do have some pull with the force. Want me to give them a call and get back to you?"

"If you want," said Jenny. "Don't go to any trouble on my account."

"No trouble," said Bolivia, smelling a story.

Bolivia pulled up on the front lawn of Sandy's cottage in Coconut Grove and turned off the motor. She found Sandy around back on her patio.

"What are you sitting back here for?" asked Bolivia.

"I like it out here," said Sandy.

"But you've got air-conditioning!"

"Do you have any idea what electricity costs? Go on in and fix yourself a drink."

When Bolivia came back outside, a can of beer in her hand, Sandy said, "I don't think we should be sneaking behind Annie's back like this."

"What're you talking about?"

"I just don't think we should."

"I didn't come over here to talk about Annie's wedding," said Bolivia. "I have a favor to ask."

"What kind of a favor?"

"A police favor, okay?" When she didn't get an argument from Sandy, she told her about Jenny's husband. "I just thought maybe you could check and see if anything's being done with the missing person's report."

"And then you want to discuss bridesmaids' dresses."

"You're wrong," said Bolivia. "That's about the last thing I want to talk about. I'd be happy if I never heard another word about bridesmaids and pink dresses and weddings."

"We can't let her down," said Sandy.

"I don't want to discuss it."

"We have to discuss it. We're her best friends, and it's the least we can do for her."

"I thought I'd get her a microwave."

"That's really nice, Bolivia."

"They're really good for heating up croissants."

"You can cook in them, too."

"What're you getting her?"

"I haven't thought about it yet. It seems like Jack has just about everything in his house already."

"Does he have a microwave?"

"I don't think so."

"Well, that's what I'm getting her."

"Maybe I'll get her sheets," said Sandy. "She probably doesn't want to sleep on the same sheets he used with that other woman."

"It hasn't bothered her so far."

"White, all-cotton sheets. The kind I'll never buy for myself because they're too expensive."

"How much can sheets cost?"

"Hundreds of dollars," said Sandy.

"You're kidding? For sheets? I just get mine at K-Mart."

"Oh, well," said Sandy, in a tone that suggested Bolivia didn't know anything about sheets.

She knew one thing. You didn't need sheets when you slept in a hammock. "Look, I don't feel like talking about this domestic stuff," said Bolivia. "It's depressing. Can't you go in the house and call Missing Persons for me?"

"As long as I'm on the phone, do you want me to order a pizza?"

"Sure. No anchovies."

"Don't you think I know that by now? And when are you going to grow up and try them, anyway?"

"Never," said Bolivia.

When Sandy came back she looked puzzled. "Something strange," she said.

"Did you order the pizza?"

"Not about that. We were told by the government not to pursue the missing person's report."

"What government?"

"*Our* government."

"City hall? What?"

"The United States government."

"The FBI?"

"Probably."

"That's weird," said Bolivia.

"They didn't even want to tell *me*. I was just told not to stick my nose in it."

"Why would they do that?"

Sandy shrugged. "Could be he's working for the government, possibly undercover. He could be in their witness protection program."

"In that case, his wife would know about it."

"Where did she say he worked?"

"She didn't. She just said they wouldn't take her calls. They haven't lived here long, though."

"That sounds like witness protection."

"Sandy, if that were the case, she'd be running to the government for help, not to me."

"What're you going to do?"

"I don't know. Probably interview her again."

"I think you'd better stay out of it, Bolivia."

"This could be a great story."

"I don't get it. None of it makes sense."

It didn't make any sense to Bolivia, either. And things that didn't make sense always drove her nuts until she figured them out. Right now, though, all she felt like was some pizza.

After getting Jenny Waring's address from Sandy, who got it off the missing person's report, Bolivia rode out to Miami Shores the next morning to interview Jenny.

# Betrayed

Miami Shores was a pretty area just north of Biscayne Boulevard, but also a paranoid area. Partial road blocks had been put up to discourage outsiders from driving through, and practically every house had security gates on the windows. It was a high crime area when it came to burglaries, but so was any middle or upper-class neighborhood in Dade County.

Bolivia swung around the road blocks, keeping an eye open for the street she wanted. When she found the address she was looking for, it was a smaller house than its neighbors, perfectly ordinary looking, but it also had the requisite bars at the windows and a security sticker on the front door.

Bolivia rang the bell. When no one answered she rang it again, then got out her notebook and pen in order to leave a note for Jenny to get in touch with her.

She was just sticking the note in the mailbox when a woman called out from the house next door.

"No one's there."

Bolivia stepped off the stoop and looked in the direction from which the voice had come. "I'm looking for Jenny Waring."

"She's not home."

"Do you know where she is?"

The woman came halfway across her front lawn to get a better look at Bolivia. "Are you a friend of hers?"

"Yes."

"I think something strange is going on," said the woman, coming closer and lowering her voice.

"Like what?"

"Two men came late last night and took her away with them."

"You mean with force?"

"Not exactly, but it didn't look to me as though she wanted to go with them."

"What did they look like?"

"Businessmen, but it was after midnight. I was just letting the cat in or I wouldn't have seen them. They each had her by an arm, and she wasn't struggling or anything, but she still didn't look like she wanted to go."

"And she hasn't been back since?"

The woman shook her head. "She didn't even have her purse with her. I knew there was something strange, but I didn't think of it until just now. That was it. You just don't walk out of the house without taking your purse."

Bolivia, who didn't even own a purse, didn't think that was strange at all. She took one of her cards out of her pocket and handed it to the woman. "Would you call me if anyone else comes around the house?"

The woman's mouth dropped open. "You're Bolivia Smith?"

Bolivia nodded.

"Oh, I love your column."

"Thank you."

"My name is Edna Worley."

"Well, thank you for talking to me, Mrs. Worley."

"Ms."

"And give me a call if you hear anything."

"Oh, I will. I'll keep an eye out, don't you worry."

Bolivia rode over to the nearest shopping center on Biscayne and found a pay phone. She called Sandy and found her still at the station.

"Something really funny's going on here," she told Sandy.

"Hi, Bolivia."

"I mean it. Two men came in the middle of the night and took Jenny Waring away with them."

"Maybe they were relatives."

"I don't think so. Her neighbor thought it was suspicious, too."

"I already told you, Bolivia, there's nothing I can do about it."

"Citizens can just be kidnapped and the police won't do anything about it? That might make an interesting column."

"You don't have a shred of proof that it's a kidnapping."

"No, but I'm going to get it."

"Fine."

"I'm going to break into her house. What I was wondering is, would you go with me?"

"No, I will not go with you, and you are not going to break the law."

Bolivia hung up on her.

It was easy enough to break in, because the back door was unlocked. Bolivia couldn't find anything that looked the least bit suspicious, though. The kitchen was ultra neat, with nothing left out. Bolivia noted that it contained a microwave. Everyone seemed to have a microwave these days. There wasn't a TV set on, or a stereo. Nothing was overturned, which would have suggested a struggle. No handbag was lying around. It was just an orderly house that looked as though its owner had momentarily stepped out.

Bolivia was also about to step out when she heard the siren. She looked out the front window just in time to see Sandy and her partner getting out of an unmarked car.

She couldn't believe it. Her best friend was going to arrest her?

Bolivia refused them the satisfaction of going out the back way and making a run for it. Instead she opened the front door and waited for Sandy and Joe Cruz.

"We going to arrest her?" Joe asked Sandy.

"Hi, guys," said Bolivia.

"So far we got breaking and entering," said Joe.

"You want me to do a column about you and your female friends, Joe?" asked Bolivia. "I'm sure your wife would enjoy reading it."

Joe just laughed. "Yeah, like that's really news," he said.

"I don't find this amusing," said Sandy.

"Look, I told you I was going to do it," said Bolivia. "It's not like I'm sneaking around. Anyway, the back door wasn't even locked and I happen to know the person who lives here."

"Put the cuffs on her, Joe," said Sandy, turning away.

"Hey, wait a minute," said Bolivia, stepping back inside and trying to slam the door.

Joe pushed his way in. "She's just kidding you," said Joe. "The last thing we feel like doing is writing up a report."

"Look, as long as you're here, would you guys take a look around? I didn't see anything suspicious, but you two have had more experience."

"We could get in trouble just being here," said Sandy.

"Pretend you didn't tell me," said Joe, "and I'll take a quick look."

Sandy ignored her while Joe looked around, and when he came back he was eating a piece of cheese. Seeing Sandy's look he said, "Hey, it was just going to go bad."

"Let's get out of here," said Sandy.

"That's it? You guys aren't going to do anything?" asked Bolivia.

"As far as I know, there's no crime," said Sandy. "If you want to pursue it for your newspaper, go right ahead."

She would pursue it, all right. She'd get to the truth if she had to go all the way back to Fort Lauderdale and shake it out of Tooley.

Which didn't sound like a half-bad idea.

## Chapter 5

"I really think I'm on to something, Henry." She tried to sound offhand, the way the men sounded when they sensed a story, but her excitement kept breaking through.

"Forget it, Bolivia."

"Henry, something very strange is going on here."

"Why, because a woman whose husband left her went out with a couple of men?"

"You make it sound like a date. You don't go out on a date with two men in the middle of the night."

"How an investigative reporter can be so naive—"

"I'm not naive, Henry. Okay, so I'll concede that it's minutely possible that Jenny Waring went out on a date with two men late at night without even carrying a handbag. Although if you saw that happening on a TV movie, Henry, I bet you wouldn't think it was so innocent."

"I don't watch TV movies."

"If you did."

"Maybe she's taken up hooking to support herself."

A typical male answer. Males assumed that all women secretly wished to be hookers. "She isn't the type."

Henry chuckled. "As I said, Bolivia, you're pretty naive at times."

"Okay, so she's a hooker," said Bolivia. "What I'm saying, Henry, is something suspicious is going on or the government wouldn't have put a clamp on the missing person's report, and I think it has something to do with that jungle camp in Lauderdale."

"That area you call a jungle camp could be a lot of things," said Henry. "It could be a training camp for Contras. It could be some of the militant Cubans planning another invasion. Or it could be exactly what it appears to be: just another place where veterans drop out of society and congregate."

"I didn't see any Cubans or Nicaraguans in there. I saw a redheaded giant, and the last time I saw him he was distinctly unfriendly."

"I wouldn't be friendly, either, if I was trying to get away from it all and some reporter kept showing up. When are you going to learn, Bolivia, that no one likes reporters? Except maybe other reporters, and I'm not even sure about that."

"Don't you even want to know if it's Cubans or Nicaraguans?"

"That's not news, Bolivia. That goes on all the time."

"Well, I don't see why I can't follow it up."

"Follow *what* up? The husband's gone, the wife's gone, what's left to follow up?"

What she wanted to follow up was why Tooley had been so unfriendly to her the second time, but she knew Henry wasn't about to buy that. "I'd just like to find Jenny Waring, see if she's all right."

"Fine. Do it on your own time. On my time, I'd like to see a column on the current unrest in Overtown."

"Yes, boss."

"And, Bolivia?"

"What?"

"Smile when you say *boss*."

*As she entered the clearing, everything had changed. Instead of a camp fire there was a waterfall. Instead of tents there was a small house made of bamboo. And instead of a group of men there was just Tooley.*

*He wheeled up to meet her, his eyes sending off green sparks. He wore a tank top that revealed his massive chest and upper arms that could crush a person. His mouth was moving sideways a little, and the tip of his tongue flicked out to wet his lower lip.*

*"I knew you would return," he said, and his voice was warm and lazy.*

*"I had to," admitted Bolivia, feeling a quickening of her blood.*

*"If you hadn't, I would have come after you."*

*His eyes were running along the length of her slim body as if memorizing its lines. She felt herself swaying toward him and shook her head a little to try to regain control.*

*"What happened?" asked Bolivia. "Everything's changed."*

*"I created this for us," said Tooley. "Our own Garden of Eden."*

*He reached for her hand and led her over to the waterfall, and now she could see the sparkling stream that was hidden behind it. As though he had issued a command, she found herself taking off her clothes. As each item of clothes dropped to the ground, she sensed Tooley's growing approval. And when she was at last naked, lovely and tan and feeling at one with nature, Tooley reached out, and rough hands began to caress her body.*

*When the heat built up to an incendiary level, she stepped into the stream until the water was up to her waist. She beckoned for him to join her, and almost in an instant he was out of his clothes and beside her in the water.*

*Where before he had seemed confined to his wheelchair, now he seemed free. He swam circles around her with bold strokes of his arms, swimming around and around like a shark circling its prey.*

*He was tempting her now, taunting her, staying just beyond her reach. She wanted to feel that wet, red, matted hair against her skin, but every time she moved in his direction he eluded her.*

*She began turning around in the water, following him with her eyes, until she became dizzy from the circling. Just as she began to fall, he caught her with strong arms, and then his body was up against hers, pressing closer and closer, almost melding with hers, and then, finally, he was entering her. And as jungle birds sang and monkeys cried out, Bolivia experienced the truest, the most profound—*

"Hey, Smith, are you playing with us or what?"

Bolivia came back to reality with a jolt, seeing the ball fly past her and go for an easy double. A chorus of groans rose from the rest of the infield.

Bolivia's mind was everywhere but on the ball that night. Top of the seventh an easy pop-up fly came her way and she missed it. Then she overthrew third, and the other team scored. Plus she struck out every time she got up to bat.

By the end of the game even her best friends were giving her the cold shoulder. Things didn't loosen up until after the second drink at the local watering hole when Anne finally said, "Something bothering you, Bolivia?"

"A whole lot of things," said Bolivia.

"Is being in my wedding making you that unhappy?"

"It's not you," Sandy said to Anne. "It's me. I almost had her arrested this morning."

Anne looked startled for a moment, then grinned at Bolivia. "Well, if you need a lawyer..."

"The whole thing's driving me nuts," said Bolivia. "Her husband disappears, then she disappears, and something's not kosher in that jungle camp."

Anne put her arm around Bolivia's shoulder. "You know, I know what's bothering you, Bollie. You're in love and you don't know it."

"And you've crossed the line into insanity," said Bolivia. The *Bollie* part was bad enough; the *love* part was patently ridiculous.

Anne gave her a smug look. "I was the same way when I was falling in love with Jack and denying it to myself. I don't think I got a hit the entire time."

"That's 'cause you're lousy at bat," said Bolivia.

"If you recall, I batted over three hundred last year."

"She did," agreed Sandy.

"I'm not in love, I'm just confused," said Bolivia.

Anne nodded. "That's exactly how I felt."

Bolivia glared at Anne. "You're really starting to tick me off, Annie."

"I know."

"Look, I'm a reporter on the trail of a hot story, and no one's cooperating. Sandy comes after me in a cop car, my boss tells me to forget it, and you accuse me of falling in love. Just because *you're* in love doesn't mean it's catching."

"Denial," said Anne. "I know what you're going through. I told myself it was the case, and you're telling yourself it's the story. But the bottom line is, you've got something going for that redhead in the jungle."

"She's got the hots for him," said Sandy.

Trying to be honest with herself, Bolivia asked herself if that was true. Well, maybe marginally, but solving riddles bothered her a lot more than sexy men did. Sexy, unfriendly men, in particular.

"I'm not denying there was a certain attraction there," said Bolivia. "In other circumstances I could probably be attracted to him."

"She's a goner," said Anne. "That's exactly what I felt."

"I don't know," said Sandy. "I've never known Bolivia to become fixated on a guy. A slight case of lust, yes, but even that never lasts long."

"It had to happen sometime," said Anne.

"I've got a great idea for you, Annie," said Bolivia. "Why don't you quit the legal business and set yourself up as a marriage broker? It seems to interest you more."

"You are getting a bit hard to take," murmured Sandy.

"What was that?" said Anne.

"It's just that since you're getting married," said Sandy, "you seem to think we should follow suit."

"I thought you wanted to get married?" said Anne.

"That's not the point," said Sandy. "The point is, all I ever meet are cops and criminals. And I don't want to marry either one."

"And I don't want to get married at all," said Bolivia.

"You just don't want to get married because of your parents," said Anne.

Bolivia nodded. "I think that's a pretty valid reason."

Anne said, "Well, I say, either go after this guy or forget about him. But really, Bolivia, have you thought about how you're going to date a guy who lives in a jungle?"

"I don't want to date him," said Bolivia. "I just want to find out what's going on."

"I don't want to hear about you breaking into any more houses," said Sandy.

Bolivia groaned. "I thought you guys would agree with me. I go out for a drink with my two best friends, I've got a problem, and all you're doing is harassing me."

"Oh, hell, and I wanted to get you in a good mood," said Anne.

Bolivia decided it was time for another drink.

"What is it?" asked Sandy. "Another dress?"

"Never mind, this isn't a good time," said Anne.

"It's never going to be a good time," said Sandy.

Bolivia tried to ignore them. Maybe if she ignored them, the conversation would go away.

"What're you guys doing Friday night?" asked Anne.

"Why?" asked Sandy.

"Since when do you ask 'why' first?" Anne asked.

"Since now," said Sandy.

"Forget it, I won't get married," said Anne, ordering herself another drink.

Sandy ordered one, too. "Come on, Annie, quit being a martyr. What do you have in mind for Friday night?"

"I just thought we could meet at Neiman Marcus and then eat in one of the restaurants at Bal Harbour."

Bolivia groaned, more loudly this time.

"The restaurant sounds all right," said Sandy. "Why Neiman Marcus?"

"She's going to show us her china pattern," said Bolivia.

"I don't need to see your china pattern," said Sandy. "Bolivia and I already know what we're getting you, and it isn't china."

Anne persevered against adversity. "I saw the perfect dresses for you there, but you need to try them on in case they need alterations."

"I can't afford Neiman Marcus," said Bolivia, thinking that would settle the issue.

"I'm paying for them," said Anne.

"You shouldn't have to pay for them," said Sandy.

"I'm paying for them because I want to," said Anne, "and that's that."

"What does this thing look like?" asked Sandy.

Anne tossed off half her beer before replying. "It doesn't have puffed sleeves, it doesn't have any bows and it isn't pink. Okay?"

"Maybe you could be a little more specific," said Sandy.

"I thought I'd go for a monochromatic look," said Anne. "I'll be in cream, you'll be in tan."

"Tan?" asked Bolivia.

"Yes, tan. Which is what you wear all the time, anyway, only you call it khaki."

"I don't know," said Sandy.

"You're both dark," said Anne, "it'll be very flattering."

"What does it look like?" asked Sandy.

"Simple," said Anne. "Sleeveless, mock turtleneck, slightly flared skirt. I've looked everywhere, and it's the plainest thing I've seen. They're not even bridesmaids' dresses."

"What goes on our heads?" asked Bolivia.

"Straw hats," said Anne. "And I thought, since you object to flowers so much, you could carry bouquets of leaves."

"Are you serious?" asked Sandy.

"No," said Anne. "That was a joke. They'll be the plainest flowers I can find, though."

"I guess that sounds all right," said Sandy.

Bolivia tried to think of something she could object to, but if she had to be a bridesmaid, it sounded about as good as it was going to get. "Yeah, I guess," she said.

"You're enthusiasm's overwhelming," said Anne.

"What kind of shoes?" asked Sandy.

"You can wear heels," said Anne, "and Bolivia can wear her hiking boots."

"I'll wear flats," said Bolivia.

"Fine," said Anne, "Then we'll meet there at six?"

"Okay with me," said Sandy.

"Sure," Bolivia agreed.

Anne's face relaxed in a smile. "Great. Drink up, it's on me."

Bolivia woke up the next morning with every intention of riding to Overtown and seeing what was up. She moved her hammock inside, took a tepid shower and washed her hair, dressed in freshly laundered khakis and walked over to the drugstore in Surfside to have breakfast and read the paper.

She was still intending to go when she went back to the parking lot of the hotel and started up her motorcycle. She was still intending it when she got to I-95, only instead of turning south to Overtown she turned north and found herself heading for Fort Lauderdale.

You're acting crazy, she told herself, but her subconscious was set on one direction even though her conscious self was telling her another. *There's nothing to find up there. He's not going to be any happier to see you than he was last time, and you don't even have an excuse to be there.* So what? she replied to herself. So she made a fool of herself; it wouldn't be the first time. And maybe she'd get lucky and really get a story.

Sure, and maybe she'd get lucky and Annie would call off the wedding. Fat chance!

She entered the jungle environs by means of the same path. She walked slowly and steadily: slowly because she hadn't thought of an excuse to give Tooley yet about why she was there; steadily because she was afraid that if she paused, she'd chicken out.

She tried out, *Tooley, I'd like to do a follow-up story, maybe get the backgrounds of some of the guys,* only it didn't wash. He wasn't stupid. He'd know that she knew that they weren't about to blab about their backgrounds to her so that they could wind up in the newspaper for anyone to read.

She improvised, *Tooley, I'm really worried because now Buddy's wife has also disappeared,* but that wasn't any better. He'd tell her to go to the police and quit bothering him.

She played around with, *Tooley, I suspect something funny is going down here, and I think the government is involved,* but the big problem with that was that if it were true, Tooley was probably government, too, and likely to have her arrested for sticking her nose in.

She tentatively ran through, *Tooley, I'm having a party Saturday night and I was wondering if you'd like to come*. The trouble with that one was that it would make her look like a world-class idiot. And she wasn't about to make herself look like an idiot to a man on purpose.

She was working on the direct approach, the honest approach, just walking into the jungle camp and summoning up her sexiest smile and keeping her fingers crossed that the attraction was mutual, when it occurred to her that she had already been walking about twice the amount of time it had previously taken her to get to the camp, and so far she hadn't seen anything remotely resembling a clearing.

Bolivia stopped and looked around. Path to the front, path behind her, jungle on both sides. She decided to assume the easiest explanation, that her sense of time was way off, probably due to the fact that her mind had been wandering. Anyway, any other explanation made no sense at all.

She did, however, check her watch, so that when another twenty minutes had passed, she knew she wasn't imagining it: something was seriously wrong. How could an entire clearing disappear? She began to experience a sense of déjà vu, then realized it was very much like a recurring dream she had had as a child where she'd be walking home from school, but no matter how far she walked, she never got any closer to home.

She thought of turning back, but not very seriously. One thing a reporter never did was give up or turn back. She was determined to keep going until she found Tooley and his men, and if she didn't find them, at least she ought to be coming out of the jungle sometime soon.

On the other hand, the trees could go on for miles as far as she knew. It could turn dark, and she'd still be walking down a path in a jungle. She didn't have a flashlight, she didn't have any water, and now that she thought about it she suddenly felt an overwhelming thirst. She didn't even have a tissue with her in case she had to make a side trip into the jungle, and, worst of all, she didn't have any insect repellent. In fact, other than her keys in her front pocket and her wallet in the back, she didn't have anything with her except the clothes she was wearing.

So was she about to panic? Hell, no. She wanted an assignment to Beirut, didn't she? Surely she could survive a hike in what was probably considered the suburbs of Fort Lauderdale.

She had to ask herself a serious question though: Was Tooley worth it?

That wasn't an easy one to answer. If it turned out to be a great story, then, yes, he was worth it. If it didn't turn out to be a story at all, but he was glad to see her, then again, yes, it was worth it.

It wasn't love, as Annie claimed. Hell, no one fell in love that fast, especially with a man who was probably lying about everything. Lust? No, not exactly. Okay, so she'd had a few lustful thoughts; she was human, wasn't she? And he was the sexiest man she had come across in at least two-and-a-half years, maybe more. She thought the correct word for what she was feeling was *possibility*. With Tooley there seemed to be the possibility of something. She hadn't felt anything like that in a long time, at least not about anything but work.

There were problems, of course. Huge problems. Perhaps insurmountable problems. (1) He had dropped out of society. (2) She had no intention of joining him in his dropping out venture. (3) He could have deserted a wife and six children for all she knew, and she didn't go after married men. Not ever. Not even red-haired beauties. (4) The wheelchair. That was something of a problem. Not as big a problem as she had thought at first, at least not in her fantasies, but a problem nonetheless. First of all, she was an active person. She liked to ride her cycle; she liked to windsurf; she liked to play baseball and volleyball in good weather and squash when it rained. And second of all, well, there was the problem of sex. Sure she had seen *Coming Home*, but it hadn't been one of her favorite movies. (5) There was a possibility he was government. If he was, forget it. Anything the government was playing around with covertly in a jungle, she didn't approve of. She didn't mind reporters sneaking around, but she didn't want the government doing it. (6) There was always the possibility that Tooley was crazy. He didn't appear to be, but there were sociopaths all over the place who seemed to be sane. For all she knew, he killed young women and buried them in the jungle.

She checked her watch again. Twenty more minutes. She should have been somewhere by now, something should have changed. She could have been walking around in circles for all she knew, and perhaps she should have paid attention to where the sun was. Only she couldn't exactly tell where the sun was, because the jungle closed so thickly over her head that barely any light got through.

And great, just what she needed, now she was walking into a swarm of mosquitoes. She tried to remember when the last case of malaria had been reported in Florida, but gave it up when all her attention became focused on trying to kill as many mosquitoes as she could in the shortest time possible.

She decided to give herself ten more minutes. If she hadn't reached the clearing—any clearing—in ten more minutes, she was going to give up and turn around. She was willing to walk miles in the heat and humidity in order to see Tooley once more, but she wasn't willing to be eaten alive by mosquitoes.

Fortunately, the mosquitoes didn't seem to be following her. She had invaded their swarm and they had bitten her, but they had stayed where they were. Of course, if she turned back, she would no doubt run into them again. She wished she hadn't figured that out.

With two minutes to go, and almost anxious by this time to turn back, she heard the first rifle shots. Acting from instinct rather than common sense, she threw herself to the ground. Only when she was spitting dirt out of her mouth did she realize that the shots were coming from some distance ahead of her, and it wasn't likely that she was the target. Especially since shots were still being fired, and they sounded more like rifle practice than hunting.

She got to her feet and brushed herself off. Her adrenaline had kicked in, and she was feeling the kind of excitement that she heard war correspondents felt. Maybe it wasn't a war, maybe she wasn't in the jungle of Southeast Asia, but it still felt exciting to her. She was alone and possibly in danger, and she loved it. She wished she could duplicate the feeling whenever she needed a lift. It was better than a drink. It was better then hitting a home run and winning the game for her team. It was almost better than good sex.

She was still feeling a high when the path took a turn and she was suddenly in a clearing. A large clearing. A really large clearing. And the clearing was filled with what seemed like hundreds of men, all in combat gear, and apparently playing war games. At least she hoped it was war games and she hadn't stumbled into a real war that no one had bothered to tell her about.

After the first stunned moment she quickly backed up, hoping to hide within the mangroves and see what was going on, wishing she had brought her camera. Just as she turned to dive out of view she found herself being tackled to the ground, this time getting more than a little dirt in her mouth.

Rough hands grabbed her and yanked her to her feet; then she was being dragged back into the clearing. She tried to fight them off, her feet kicking out, throwing her weight behind her shoulders to get out of their grasp, turning and twisting and wishing she had learned a martial art instead of opting for squash lessons.

She didn't recognize the men holding on to her. They were wearing helmets, and they looked like they had black paint under their eyes, the way football players did, but she didn't think she had ever seen them before.

She tried cursing them out, which usually got at least a chuckle from men, but these guys didn't have a sense of humor. At least she didn't give them the satisfaction of screaming. Not that it would have done any good.

The men were up off the ground now and watching her being dragged forward. They started to back off, giving the guys room to drag her through their midst, and at the far end of the clearing, all alone, a giant of a man was watching their progress. He was wearing a helmet like the others, and camouflage gear, his arms were crossed, and she had a feeling he wasn't happy. She thought of shouting out for Tooley, but immediately after thinking that she realized the man *was* Tooley.

Tooley. Standing up. Not only on perfectly healthy legs, but legs that looked like tree trunks. The guy had to be six foot six, minimum, to tower over the other men the way he was doing.

And then she saw something else, something almost as strange as Tooley standing on his own feet: next to Tooley stood the man whose picture Jenny Waring had shown her.

The two men holding her thrust her in front of Tooley and twisted her arms behind her back. She stood as tall as she could, but she still had to look up at him. She felt instantly at a disadvantage, more so than even being held in place by the two men. It was a rare occasion when she had to look up at a man.

Knowing that a good offense was a great defense Bolivia said, "What the hell do you think you're doing?"

"Secure her," ordered Tooley.

## Chapter 6

"Secure me? Are you crazy? I'm a reporter," yelled Bolivia, trying to kick Tooley and missing him.

"What better reason?" he asked.

"My newspaper knows where I am, and so do the police."

"Save your breath, Bolivia, you aren't going anywhere."

She tried a smile. "Look, Tooley, can't we come to some sort of compromise? You let me go and I'll forget I've ever been here."

"You're asking me to trust a reporter?"

Bolivia tried to look trustworthy.

"Forget it," said Tooley. "This time you've seen too much."

Bolivia tried to kick him again in frustration. "Why don't you just shoot me?"

"No need to get so dramatic. You'll just be paying us a short visit, that's all."

"It better be short, because I'm expected somewhere in an hour. And if I don't show up..."

Tooley ignored her.

"Just one question," said Bolivia. "Am I crazy, or did that clearing you were in before disappear?"

"We camouflaged it," said Tooley, "to keep people like you out. Tie her up in the wheelchair," he ordered the men, the hint of a smile playing around his mouth.

"Did a miracle happen," asked Bolivia, "and you could suddenly walk?"

Tooley grinned. "No one notices a guy in a wheelchair. You hardly even get acknowledged."

Which was probably true, but Bolivia had noticed him. She guessed it was as good a disguise as any, though, particularly if you wanted to look ineffectual.

One of the men wheeled over Tooley's chair, minus the rifle in the back, and Bolivia was thrust into the seat. While she tried to fight them off, they tied her wrists to the arms and her ankles to the footrest. She found the loss of control devastating.

As Tooley walked away, the men following him, Bolivia shouted, "You can't just leave me here."

Tooley turned around and seemed to reconsider. "You're right," he finally said. "Wheel her a little way into the brush, guys, so we don't have to listen to her bitching."

Bolivia desperately looked around until she spotted Jenny Waring's husband in the crowd. "You, Eldon," she said, "do you know your wife had the police looking for you?"

The man turned his back on her.

"Did you know she's disappeared?" Bolivia yelled.

"On second thought," said Tooley, "gag her. I'm sure that mouth of hers can be heard a mile from here."

Bolivia started to protest, but already one of the men had taken a scarf from around his neck, and while the other one held her head, the gag was slipped between her teeth. Too furious by now to speak anyway, Bolivia silently fumed as she was wheeled down the path a few yards and then abandoned.

She tested the ropes to see if there was any slack that bound her, but there wasn't. She rocked her body to see if the momentum could propel the wheelchair forward, but it wouldn't budge. They had probably locked the wheels.

In one last effort to free herself she hurtled her body to the side. The wheelchair slowly toppled over, finally catching on the undergrowth so that she was halfway to the ground.

The position couldn't be worse.

It was several hours later when the wheelchair was jerked upright and she felt herself being wheeled down the path away from the clearing. She turned her head and saw that a man she didn't recognize was wheeling her.

Maybe he was going to wheel her out of the jungle and back to civilization. If they thought they were going to get away with this treatment of her, they had another think coming. She was sore all over. The ropes had stopped the blood from circulating in her legs and arms, her throat was so dry she wondered if she'd be able to talk, and she was very sorry she'd had so many cups of coffee that morning. They were going to be even sorrier; she was going to have the police on them in nothing flat.

The path turned, then turned again, and she was wheeled into a third clearing. This one had the large orange tent and the smaller pup tents, but it also had a mess tent where she could see food being cooked and, off to one side, folding tables and chairs were set up. It looked like some damn Boy Scout camp.

Bolivia was wheeled over to the orange tent and deposited outside. Several moments later, Tooley emerged.

"Gotten control of your temper yet?" he asked her.

Bolivia narrowed her eyes and tried to turn him to stone with her thoughts.

"Still simmering, I see," he said. He folded his arms and looked down at her, his head tilted to one side. "Well, you're a sorry sight, but I suppose you know that."

In a fit of temper, Bolivia flung herself to the side again and sent the wheelchair crashing to the ground. Now she was sore in places she hadn't been before. And instead of Tooley rushing to her rescue, he was laughing at her.

"Interesting move," said Tooley. "Although what you thought you'd accomplish by it, I don't know."

She couldn't imagine what she had ever found attractive about him. He was an ignorant, unfeeling animal, and if he dropped dead on the spot she would sigh with relief.

Tooley bent down and righted the wheelchair with one hand. "You're causing me a problem, Bolivia."

She rolled her eyes.

"We're not set up for women in here. I'd like to untie you and let you go in search of some privacy in case you're feeling the call of nature, but I'm afraid I don't trust you out of my sight."

Well, not totally ignorant.

"I'm going to ask you a question now, Bolivia, and a lot is going to depend on your answer. If I take off the gag, do you think you can control that mouth of yours? Just nod your head yes or no."

She stubbornly shook her head.

"That's what I figured. I also figure you must be thirsty by this time, and I don't plan on starving you to death—particularly since you're skinny enough as it is—but you're going to stay there, gag in place, until I get some assurance from you that you'll behave yourself."

Bolivia stared at a point somewhere above his head.

"I'll tell you what. I don't have all day to stand around here, and you can't very well yell at me when you've changed your mind, so we'll use that little trick of yours. When you decide you want to join us in some chow—and that's with the stipulation that you promise to behave yourself—just throw yourself over in the wheelchair again. That'll be the signal."

She was still facing his tent as he walked off. She could hear talking and laughter from the men and smell some kind of meat being barbecued. *Skinny?* He thought she was skinny? Well, she'd rather be emaciated than eat a meal with him. She'd sit in the wheelchair until he had to take her out, dead or alive. She'd be damned if she'd give him the satisfaction of watching her topple over again. Promise to behave herself? Fat chance!

"Good chow," said Tooley. "Too bad you had to miss out on it."

He was looking down at her again, a habit that was really beginning to annoy her. She had preferred it when he was the one in the wheelchair. A large cigar was between the thumb and first finger of his left hand, and he was looking full and satisfied.

"Obviously, you're too stubborn to know what's good for you. Luckily for you I'm not as childish as you are or I'd let you sit there until you became insect food."

He made a move in her direction, and she threw her head back.

*Betrayed*

"What do you think," said Tooley, waving his cigar, "this is torture time? I'm just enjoying an after meal smoke. No need to flinch." He puffed on the cigar, and some of the smoke drifted her way. She had smelled worse. In fact, she had once tried cigar smoking herself, thinking it was a very reporter kind of thing to do. She had liked the image, but she hadn't liked the taste.

Tooley said, "Now here's what I'm going to do, so you'll be prepared. I'm going to have your hands tied behind your back, a rope tied around your waist, and then you're going to be allowed into the brush on your own, rather like a dog on a leash, and you better take advantage of this little rest period because you're not going to get another one until tonight. Your privacy will be assured. You can take my word for it."

Bolivia flung the chair over on its side again. At the rate she was abusing it, it probably wouldn't be good for much when she was through with it.

Tooley seemed to enjoy the sight. "Well, now, let me think," he said. "Was that a display of temper, or were you telling me you could be trusted with the gag off?"

Bolivia managed to nod her head in the dirt.

"Does that mean you want the gag off?"

She nodded again and glared at him at the same time.

He squatted down beside her and took the gag out of her mouth. Bolivia tried to swallow, but couldn't manage it. She found she was able to talk, though.

"You can't tie my hands behind my back," she said.

"I assure you I can," said Tooley.

"If I'm going to be allowed to relieve myself," said Bolivia, "then I need my hands free in order to get my pants down."

"Clear, concise thinking," said Tooley. "That must come from being a reporter. I guess what we'll have to fashion is some kind of a harness. Rather like you used to see little kids in. Just hold tight here for a few minutes and I'll see if I can come up with something."

*"Get me up off the ground!"* screamed Bolivia.

Bushy red eyebrows lowered until his eyes looked at half mast. "Did you yell at me, Bolivia?"

"I'm flat against an ant hill."

"You'll be flat against an ant hill with a gag in your mouth if you don't apologize to me for that outburst and assure me it won't happen again."

Bolivia looked at the ants and then looked at Tooley. "In a pig's eye," she told him.

The gag was put back in place.

Gagged and harnessed, Bolivia was allowed twenty-five feet of rope to find herself a private place. Ten feet proved enough for her, and with relief so great it overcame the conditions, she took advantage of Tooley's suspect gesture. If he though this was going to endear him to her, he was wrong.

She then went the remaining fifteen feet, all the while trying to find a way out of the harness. In books people were always able to get themselves untied. If it was that easy, why couldn't she manage? For one thing, the knots were in the back, where she couldn't reach them. For another, she wasn't a contortionist.

She kept trying, though, until she felt the first hard tug on the rope, and then she was being hauled back to the camp whether she was ready or not.

She found a smiling Tooley at the other end of the rope. "Trying to escape?" he asked her.

She kicked at him, but he moved back out of her reach.

"It wouldn't have done you any good even if you had escaped," he told her. "We now have guards on every path, and they've been told to use force if you try to escape."

Bolivia decided to pretend she was a hostage in Lebanon. She would refuse to speak or to cooperate in any way; she'd just wait for a chance to escape. On the other hand, some of those hostages were still over there.

"I can see by the nasty look you just gave me that you're still not ready to have that gag removed."

On the other hand, she was dying of thirst. She used her hand to mime taking a drink of water.

"Don't tell me you're thirsty? Really?"

Bolivia could have slit his throat.

"Bobby Joe," he yelled, "bring me a canteen."

Bolivia swore she'd hold her tongue, but she couldn't help it. As soon as Tooley had the canteen in his hand and was pulling off her gag she said, "The hostages in Lebanon get treated better than this."

The gag went back in place, and the canteen of water was poured over her head. It wasn't as good as a drink, but she didn't mind it. At least her face felt cool, and it might have washed some of the dirt and sweat off.

Tooley called two of the men over and told them to take her into his tent and tie her up.

It was later, much later. She could no longer see her watch, but it seemed as though hours had passed. She had been lecturing herself. *You don't know how to get along with men, and you never did,* she told herself. *You have a big mouth, and you're abrasive, and the only one it's hurting at the moment is yourself. Tooley is clearly in charge, and you might not like that, but not liking it isn't going to change the facts.* All of which made a lot of sense but had no effect on her attitude. She was in the right; they were clearly up to no good, and she'd be damned if she was going to cooperate.

The worst of it, though—the very worst—was that she was still attracted to him. Why that was, when she couldn't stand overbearing men who acted like bullies, she didn't know. She might hate him as a person, but she was still attracted to him as a man. It didn't make any sense at all. And things that didn't make sense drove her nuts.

She had been facing the side of the tent, but now, with a painful move, she managed to roll over. The tent was dark, but she could make out a cot and a foot locker. She had no hope of Tooley giving up his cot to her tonight. Nor would she take it if it were offered. It didn't look any more comfortable than the dirt floor.

Her stomach was starting to rumble, but at least she wasn't so hungry that she had humbled herself in order to eat with them tonight. She'd had a big breakfast, enough to carry her through until tomorrow without any hardship on her part. She could sure use a cold drink, though.

When the tent flap was unzipped and a man ducked into the tent, she assumed it was Tooley. It wasn't until he spoke and she heard the Southern accent that she knew it wasn't.

"Hi, I'm Bobby Joe," said a sweet-sounding voice.

He walked over to her and knelt down beside her. "Tooley sent me in to see if you want any supper."

Bolivia shook her head.

"We sent out for some Kentucky Fried Chicken. Cole slaw, mashed potatoes, biscuits—all the works."

Her dry mouth began to salivate. My God, she was no better than a dog!

"You can come out and join us, or you can eat in here. Up to you, ma'am."

With a lot of effort and a lot of pain, Bolivia rolled away from him. She didn't like the idea that she could be bought with Kentucky Fried Chicken.

The tent turned dark again, and she could hear the noise of the flap being zipped back up.

*She was walking into a restaurant. It was the kind of restaurant with a maître d' in black tie, and silver and crystal on the tables. She was bowed to and then led to her table, the best one in the restaurant, the one that overlooked the entire city.*

*She ordered wine and then leisurely surveyed the menu. She knew she would be ordering rack of lamb; it was that kind of night.*

*The wine was poured for her; she sipped it, let it settle in the back of her throat, then nodded her satisfaction. A basket of hot rolls was placed on the table.*

*Bolivia ordered a dinner salad and a baked potato with the lamb. Later on she'd have strawberries and cream for dessert, or maybe one of the pastries they were known for.*

*The lamb was perfect; crisp on the outside and succulent and rare within. She cut herself a piece, lifted the fork to her mouth—*

"I'm back again," came the voice of Bobby Joe, shattering her fantasy. Funny, though, she could still smell food.

"I brought your supper," said Bobby Joe.

The next moment a battery operated lantern was lit, and the entire tent and Bobby Joe came into focus. He was as sweet-faced as he sounded and not much more than a boy.

He came over to her and set a tray of food in front of her. The sight of it drew her up into a sitting position, her hands tied behind her back, her ankles tied together in front of her.

"I can't untie your hands," said Bobby Joe, "so what I'm going to do is take off your gag and feed you. I'm pretty good at it. I used to feed my sister when she was little."

She was going to be fed like a baby? Well, at least it was better than being fed by Tooley.

"Nod if it's okay with you," said Bobby Joe.

The nod was instantaneous.

Bobby Joe grinned with pleasure. "I knew you'd be wanting some supper, I just knew it. The other guys teased me, but I told them Bobby Joe always gets his way."

If Tooley had said that to her, she would have rebelled. But Bobby Joe was so inoffensive he was likable.

He gently removed the gag from her mouth and lifted the Coke so that she could take a sip from the straw. It tasted better than the best champagne.

"Bobby Joe," she said, her voice coming out in a croak.

"Yes?" He smiled at her, showing crooked front teeth.

"If you help me escape, I'll pay you five hundred dollars."

The smile dimmed. "Aren't you happy here?"

"I'm serious. If you'll take a check, I'll make it more."

"I don't need any money," said Bobby Joe, looking troubled now.

"This is kidnapping. It's against the law. Do you really want to be involved in this?"

"Nobody kidnapped you, ma'am. You came here all on your own. And more than once, too."

"Is there anything I can bribe you with? How about a motorcycle?"

He ignored the question. "Now your face is going to get messy from all the grease on the fried chicken, but don't you go worrying yourself about it. I'll wipe it clean afterwards."

"Thank you," Bolivia managed to say.

"You're entirely welcome," said Bobby Joe.

He held up a drumstick, and she was just sinking her teeth into it when the tent flap was pulled back and Tooley ducked in. He remained bent over. A normal person could stand up in the tent, but that wasn't true of giants.

"She's eatin'," said Bobby Joe, looking pleased with himself. "She's behavin' like a little lamb."

"I guess she learned her lesson," said Tooley, smiling in a self-satisfied way.

In the next instant Bolivia spit out the chicken.

"Go to hell!" she roared. "And take your chicken with you!"

Bobby Joe looked flustered, and Tooley looked amused. "I think she wants her gag back," he said. "She doesn't seem to function real well without it."

When Bobby Joe went to slip the scarf back into her mouth, Bolivia bit him. He drew back with a howl, his eyes going to Tooley.

"Better go see to that wound," said Tooley. "I'll take care of the prisoner."

It had felt good to sink her teeth into someone. It was going to feel even better when it was Tooley's flesh.

Tooley sat down on the cot and leaned his arms on his knees while Bolivia contemplated spitting that distance.

"I'm going to give you a little talk," said Tooley. "Try to raise your morale." He paused a moment, as though waiting for her to interrupt him.

Bolivia scooted her rear end around on the ground until her back was to Tooley. She didn't feel like keeping quiet, but she also didn't feel like having the gag back in place so soon. She'd bide her time, try to hold back as long as she could.

"You got a choice," said Tooley. "You can either do hard time or easy time. That's a prison term, and I guess what it means is, you can either live in halfway decent circumstances with a modicum of freedom, or you can live in solitary confinement. In other words, it's up to you whether you make this painful on yourself or easy. You listening to me, Bolivia?"

She responded with a slight jerk of her head, which she figured could signify anything.

"For right now you can abandon all hope of getting out of here. You've seen too much, you've demonstrated just how very large a mouth you have, and this is just too important to risk leaking it to the press."

"Important?" muttered Bolivia. "What're you doing, invading Cuba again?"

"I'll pretend I didn't hear that," said Tooley.

"Then I'll say it louder."

"Agreeable as it may be to spar with you, Bolivia, I don't have the time at the moment. I'm trying to suppress any personal animosity I might feel towards your damn inquisitiveness in order to hammer out a working relationship with you."

"You'll have no relationship with me, working or otherwise," said Bolivia.

She heard a sigh. Then a chuckle. "You're trying my patience."

She gave a snort of derision.

"I'm going to put my cards on the table. It's getting dark, and there's the problem of where you're going to sleep. A problem, I might add, that's been the subject of conversation in this camp for the last several hours. Even now, bets are being made and straws are being drawn. I'm going to give you a choice. You can either share this two man tent with me and be under my protection, or you can have one of the pup tents and take your chances."

"I'll take my chances," retorted Bolivia.

Tooley was silent for a moment. "Perhaps I didn't word that clearly. I'm inviting you to be my guest in my tent. If you wish to decline, I can't vouch for the men's behavior. I can vouch for my own, however, and it will be impeccable."

"I'll take the pup tent," said Bolivia.

Tooley spent a moment clearing his throat. "Some of these men haven't seen a woman—"

"Baloney," said Bolivia. "You're not in Vietnam now, Tooley, you're in Fort Lauderdale. All those guys have to do is walk a few blocks to the nearest bar and they'll find all the women they could hope for. How stupid do you think I am, anyway?"

"Bobby Joe?" yelled Tooley. "Send a couple of men in here to move the prisoner."

And before Bolivia had a chance to do any more arguing, the gag was back in place.

Bolivia felt lucky she didn't have claustrophobia, because the pup tent surely would have brought it out.

It was small and low and totally dark. She couldn't get comfortable no matter what position she managed to shift to, and she could feel small things crawling over her. She was hungry, she was thirsty, the corners of her mouth were worn raw, as were her ankles and wrists, and she could swear they had put the remains of the fried chicken in the tent with her, because she could still smell it.

Nevertheless, it was the closest to a war zone she had ever gotten, and that knowledge alone buoyed her up. With just a little bit of imagination she could imagine herself as a prisoner of war plotting an escape.

It was heady stuff for a reporter who had never gotten a foreign assignment, and so far it didn't seem any more dangerous than a game. It was exactly the sort of game she had enjoyed playing as a child with the boys in the neighborhood, but, of course, in those days she had always been the one doing the tying up.

Well, that could happen again. Tooley was smart, but she was smarter, and probably ten times sneakier. He'd just better watch it when the tables got turned.

## Chapter 7

*The bed was soft and luxurious. The sheets were pristine white and one hundred percent cotton, just like the ones Sandy had told her about. There was air-conditioning, and she snuggled beneath the comforter, her head nestled in a soft pillow of down. In another room her breakfast was being prepared for her: cantaloupe, eggs, thick ham, buttered toast, a pot of coffee, all to be brought in to her on a white wicker breakfast tray. In the bathroom her whirlpool bath was being prepared so that the temperature would be just right. Soft music was playing in the background, and Bolivia felt the smile forming on her mouth, the smile that acknowledged all was right with her world..*

Someone shook her shoulder gently, and she looked up, prepared to see the arrival of her breakfast. Then reality and wakefulness appeared in the guise of Bobby Joe, who had crawled into her pup tent and was prostrate beside her.

"Tooley wants to see you in his tent," he said.

She couldn't seem to let go of her dream. Would there be any breakfast for her? Just toast and coffee would do.

"Let me help you," said Bobby Joe, reaching out and putting his hands on her upper arms and giving a tug.

She shook her head violently at the pain he caused to her wrists, and he let go in a hurry.

"Sorry about that," he said. "Just follow me outside the tent at a crawl, all right?"

Bobby Joe crawled out, and Bolivia remained where she was. If Tooley wanted to see her, he could damn well come here.

Bobby Joe stuck his head back in. "You couldn't?"

Bolivia shook her head.

Moments later rough hands reached in and dragged her out.

"See if you can stand up," said a man she hadn't seen before.

Bolivia ignored him.

Two men reached down and pulled her to her feet. When they let go of her, she lost her balance and tumbled to the ground.

One of the men said, "I guess you're not going to be able to go see Tooley unless I untie your ankles."

A reasonable assumption, thought Bolivia, experiencing a few more aches in a few more places.

"But I haven't been authorized to untie you. Stay right there. I'll be back in a minute."

What did he think she was going to do, run for it?

She watched the man disappear into Tooley's tent, and moments later he was back. He bent down to untie her

*Betrayed*

ankles, and then he and another man led her over to Tooley's tent. They didn't go inside, though.

Bolivia thought of shaking loose from the men and making a run for it, but she didn't think she could run. She could barely even walk.

They moved her forward to the other side of the tent, where Tooley was seated at a folding table, looking at a map. Before she could get a look at the map, he had turned it upside down. Beside it sat a tin mug full of coffee. The sight of the coffee made her instantly forget the map. The aroma alone was enough to make her feel dizzy with longing.

"Morning, Bolivia," said Tooley with a grin.

Bolivia tried to kick some dirt at him, but her ankle wasn't functioning all that well, and all she managed to do was stub her toe.

Tooley noticed her eyes on his mug and held it up in front of her. "Care for some coffee? Oh, I forgot, you can't drink with that gag on." He set the mug back down.

Bolivia's eyes went from the coffee to him, and she tried to make them imploring.

"What're you trying to tell me, Bolivia? You trying to say you had a good night's sleep?"

Her look grew more frantic.

"You want your gag off so you can thank me?"

Bolivia started to nod, then stopped halfway. Like hell she'd thank him.

"Guess you're getting attached to it," he said. "What I wanted to see you about is I was wondering if you'd like a shower."

Bolivia rolled her eyes.

"I'm serious. We have a shower rigged up. Only problem is, everyone can see you." He grinned at her for a moment and then said, "But some of the guys solved that problem. They've put some blankets around the perimeter so you can shower in privacy."

Tooley stood up and disappeared inside his tent. Bolivia looked around, wondering if she could escape, but there were men all over the place, and they all seemed to be watching her.

Tooley was back carrying a T-shirt and a pair of pants. "Here's the scenario," he said. "You shower with your clothes on—that kind of kills two birds with one stone. Then you hand your wet clothes over the top of the blanket and someone will set them out to dry. Meanwhile, you'll be given these clothes of mine to put on. The beauty of it is, we won't have to tie your ankles anymore. I figure my pants are a good foot too long for you anyway, and you won't be able to walk in them. Rendering you helpless, so to speak." His smile was wicked.

"And after your shower, if you're a good little girl, you might get some breakfast. But that depends entirely on how cooperative you are."

*Good little girl?* If she ever got out of here alive, she'd have his neck for that.

Two men led Bolivia over to the edge of the clearing. She saw a hose hanging over the branch of a tree and two blankets blocking the view. The men pushed her through the blankets, and the next thing she knew cold water was cascading out of the hose and onto her head. She lifted her face and found that the water quickly soaked the gag and some of it dripped into her mouth. It tasted like elixir.

When the water finally gave out, Tooley's head appeared over the blankets. "I guess I forgot something," said Tooley. "I'm going to have to untie your hands in order for you to get undressed and dressed. I don't figure you're going to make a run for it in the buff, though. Turn around."

Bolivia hesitated for a moment and then decided she had nothing to gain by sitting around in wet clothes all day. She turned, Tooley reached in and untied her hands, and then she slowly got out of her clothes and handed them over the blanket. She kept her wet panties on and was very glad she didn't wear a bra.

She was also glad, since she didn't have a bra, that the T-shirt was olive green. A white one could have proved embarrassing. She pulled up the pants, which were miles too big for her, then pulled the T-shirt over her head. Then she belatedly realized that she could remove her gag. She did so, feeling the sore corners of her mouth. She used the scarf as a belt to keep her pants from falling down. Tooley was right, though; she could barely walk in them.

When she pushed through the blankets Tooley was nowhere in sight. She saw that most of the men were seated at the folding tables eating breakfast. She headed in their direction, sure with every step that Tooley would show up to stop her. When she got as far as the first table and he hadn't stopped her yet, she sat down at the end of one of the benches.

"Hungry?" the guy sitting across from her asked.

"I could use a cup of coffee," she said, and a few of the men laughed. So they knew she was starving, so what? That didn't mean she had to admit it.

A cup of coffee was passed down to her, and the first thing it did was burn her tongue. The next sip, though, brought a needed jolt of caffeine to her system, and she sighed with pleasure.

She let her eyes drift to the trays on the table. The men were eating scrambled eggs and hash browns and what looked like hot muffins. It took all her control not to eat off the tray of the man beside her.

When a similar tray was set in front of her, she waited for a moment to see if it was a trick. Then someone said, "Dig in," and she obliged.

She was on her third mouthful of food, trying not to wolf it down, when a shadow appeared on her left, and she looked up to see Tooley standing there watching her.

He gave her a big smile "Glad to see you got your appetite back," he said.

Bolivia debated for a moment, and it wasn't an easy decision. But it was the right one. She picked up the tray of food and smashed it against Tooley's midsection, taking a perverse pleasure in the sight of scrambled eggs mashed into his clean clothes.

Tooley's smile remained in place. "Bobby Joe," he said, "have the men tie her up in the pup tent again. This little girl hasn't learned her lesson yet."

Then it was a contest to see how many choice words Bolivia could get out before Tooley got another scarf tied around her mouth.

She had to keep her strength up. Everything she had ever read about prisoners said they worked to keep their strength up. Of course, eating would keep her strength up, but if eating meant having to toady to Tooley, eating would have to go.

Exercise. She had to exercise. If she didn't keep fit, she wouldn't be able to make a run for it even if she got the chance. She had to keep her circulation going. She had to move her muscles. She had to do something.

It was only her arms that were tied at the moment. Tooley was figuring on his pants keeping her in place. She couldn't roll up the legs or even take them off, because her hands were tied behind her back. And the gag was back. And she had looked out the flap and seen an armed guard in front of her tent. You'd think she was Public Enemy Number One the way they were treating her.

Well, she didn't need her hands to escape, and she didn't need her mouth. All she needed was a good pair of legs, and she had that.

If she could stand up, she could run in place. But she couldn't stand up, so that was out.

She rolled over on her back, which hurt her wrists like hell. Then she slowly began to flex her ankles, trying to work some of the soreness out. After that she would do some leg lifts, and after that she could do a cycling exercise. That is, if her arms weren't broken by that point.

What else did prisoners do? For one thing they kept their minds occupied so they wouldn't go crazy. She didn't think that applied—she didn't think she'd go crazy. Maybe crazy with rage, but not the kind of crazy that prisoners in solitary worried about.

Three things kept her spirits up: (1) The idea of getting revenge on Tooley when she got out of here. (2) The fact that she'd have a great story if she ever got to write it. And (3) It was probably the best adventure she'd ever had. If this didn't prepare her for an assignment in a war zone, she didn't know what would. Henry would have to listen to her when she got out of this.

She heard the flap being unzipped and stopped flexing her ankles.

"Miss? Can I come in a minute?"

A polite voice? Obviously not Tooley. She turned around and saw a bespectacled face giving her a worried look. He was carrying a First Aid box with him.

Bolivia nodded.

The man crawled inside. "I used to be a nurse, miss. I thought I'd take a look at your wrists and ankles. Rope burns can be pretty nasty, and with the humidity down here, you're open to infection."

He seemed to be waiting for her to speak, and since she couldn't, she nodded a few times. Not that Tooley wouldn't deserve to have her die of an infection, leaving her death on his head. She, however, was not ready to die.

The man motioned for her to roll over, and she did so. He pushed up her pant legs to expose her ankles, then shook his head at the dark, red marks. She was raw there, and the wounds wouldn't seem to dry up.

He opened the box and took out some petroleum jelly and worked it gently over her skin. Then he covered the rope burns with several layers of gauze.

"You shouldn't be going barefoot," he said. "Those wounds should be kept clean."

Bolivia started to get agitated, wanting to explain to him and not being able to.

He put a hand on her shoulder to calm her down, then removed the gag from her mouth.

"He didn't give me back my shoes," she said. "I guess he thinks I can't run barefoot."

"At least a pair of socks," he said. "I'll get you some of mine when I'm through here. And I'd just as soon you didn't take another shower until those wounds dry."

"What's the point? My ankles will probably be tied up again."

"I won't allow it. Not until they heal, anyway, and then only with padding to protect your skin. My name's Mason, by the way."

"I'm Bolivia."

"Oh, we all know who you are."

"Then you know I haven't done anything wrong and I'm being kept against my will."

"If the bribe's coming next, forget it. You might as well know we're all committed to the cause."

"What cause?"

He seemed about to speak, and then smiled instead. "You reporters, always after a story."

He looked at the corners of her mouth, then patted on some petroleum jelly. "I guess we could tape up your mouth instead, but it wouldn't feel any better. Maybe worse."

"Please don't tape it," said Bolivia.

"Probably be easier on all of us if we just cut out your tongue."

Bolivia recoiled in horror, and Mason laughed. "Hey, I was only making a joke. We're soldiers, not terrorists."

Bolivia decided to let that one go.

He moved around to the back of her. "Your wrists look pretty bad," he said. "What I'm going to do is, I'm going to tie your arms around the elbows, then take care of your wrists. Then I'll fasten some padding before I tie you up again."

"Gee, thanks," said Bolivia.

"Or I can walk out of here now and let you get infected."

"Sorry."

He was just retying her wrists when Tooley stuck his head in. "How's it going, Mason?"

"She's going to get an infection, Tooley."

Tooley looked as though he'd like to join them, but there wasn't any room inside. Instead, he stared at Bolivia. She, in turn, stared studiously at the ground.

"Can you think of a more effective way of silencing her?" Tooley asked him.

"Not short of cutting out her tongue."

Tooley's eyes took on a gleam.

"Or drugging her," said Mason.

"No! No way," said Bolivia, backing into a corner of the tent.

"Nobody's going to drug you," said Mason, "for the simple reason that we don't have any drugs."

"Not that they're hard to get," Tooley said.

"That should do it for now," said Mason. "I'm just going to get her a clean pair of socks, and then she's all set."

As soon as Mason was out of the tent, Tooley crawled halfway in. "We can always leave the gag off if you change your ways."

Bolivia bit her tongue to keep from yelling at him.

"Well, isn't that sweet," said Tooley, all smiles. "I finally said something to you and didn't get smart talk in reply. Our little girl's finally learning some manners."

He started to crawl closer to her, and Bolivia took aim and spat.

Two seconds later she was gagged again.

She was going to escape tonight. She was going to escape in her panties and T-shirt, but that was okay, because it was Florida, and she would look like everyone else coming from the beach.

She refused lunch. She refused dinner. The only thing she didn't refuse was a trip into the jungle on the end of a rope to relieve herself. And the periodic drinks of water that Mason insisted she have.

On the last trip into the jungle before she was put in the tent for the night, she made sure that the scarf she used to keep her pants up was only loosely tied in the front. She waited until the sounds of the camp died down, signaling that most of the men were in the tents sleeping, and then she wiggled against the ground until Tooley's enormous pants slid off her. She kicked free of them, happy that his T-shirt hit her midthigh. Not that she would let modesty stand in the way of escaping, but she'd feel pretty stupid flagging down a car in her underpants. And she'd have to flag down a car, because Tooley now had her wallet and motorcycle keys.

She wriggled over to the flap and slowly, inch by inch, she unzipped it, making as little noise as possible. She peeked out. To her surprise she needn't have been so quiet, because there wasn't a guard in front of her tent as she had supposed. There were three men a little way off playing poker by the light of the camp fire, but the front of her tent was in darkness. She guessed they didn't think she was capable of an escape attempt. They probably thought she was too hungry and too demoralized to even try.

Well, those stupid men were going to have to revise their thinking in the morning when they found she was gone.

She slunk on her belly out of the tent, taking care to keep her head as low to the ground as possible. She edged around to the back of her tent and made it without being seen. By keeping to the backs of the next few pup tents, she would come to one of the paths. Tooley had said there were guards on every path, but she didn't believe him. And even if there were, she could go around them. She'd face anything in the jungle just to get out of here.

The ground was muddy from the usual afternoon thunderstorm. She didn't mind; the slickness enabled her to move with more ease and less pain. It seemed to take forever, but she was finally to the end of the pup tents when she heard some voices coming from the last tent in Spanish. It wasn't the Spanish that stopped her; Spanish was routinely spoken in Miami. It was what they were saying in Spanish. And what they were saying was something about an invasion of Tamoros.

She moved closer to where the voices were coming from to see if she could hear more, but all they were talking about now was the numerous amount of cases of diarrhea that had occurred after their lunch that day. Bolivia was very glad she had skipped lunch.

She eyed the path just ahead with indecision. Did she want to escape? Was the purpose of this jungle camp and all the war games an invasion of Tamoros? And if it was, what did she want to do?

For one thing, it would mean the best story of her career. Probably of a lifetime. But that meant staying, not running back to Miami and blowing the story sky-high before it even happened.

She had to stay. She had to be in on it. She had to gain Tooley's confidence and get him to take her along with them. My God, it would make her career. If she could get an exclusive, an eyewitness account, of a story like that she could write her own ticket. There would be talk shows, book contracts, offers from every major newspaper in the country.

Plus, Tamoros was news. A former French colony in the Caribbean, it had suffered for years under a repressive dictator who kept the people in poverty. When the dictator was finally ousted in a military coup, the generals had promised to set up a democracy and hold elections, but they had turned out to be as corrupt as the dictator, with a regime as repressive as the one they had banished, killing anyone and everyone who disagreed with them.

Thousands of Tamorons had fled to Miami on fishing boats and rafts and even inner tubes, many of them perishing on the way. It was an old story, but with a new twist: this time our government seemed to be getting involved. Because if Tooley and Eldon Waring and some of the others weren't government, she wasn't Smith of the *Times*.

She couldn't escape; she had to stay. She had to start behaving; she had to start lulling Tooley into thinking he had succeeded in taming her. She had to use any means it took in order to win his trust. Not that she had a problem with some of those means; now that she knew what he was up to, she was more attracted to him than ever. The idealistic side of her believed the government shouldn't be allowed to interfere in the politics of another county; the passionate side of her wanted to kick those generals off the face of the earth.

Was it likely Tooley would take her along on the invasion? No. But what else could he do? If he let her loose, she'd break the story and alert the generals. It was inconceivable that he'd resort to killing her. Maybe he'd want to, but the U.S. government didn't go around killing innocent people. And if he did take her, afterward she'd give them the kind of good publicity they couldn't buy. She might even get a medal from the president.

She slowly turned around and started to writhe back to her tent. If she got caught now she'd blow the whole thing. No one would believe she'd just gone out for a nightly crawl. Getting caught in an escape attempt might call for drastic action, such as keeping her in some safe house while the invasion went down.

She made it to the back of her tent, then slowly shimmied around the side. And there, seated in front of her tent, a rifle across his legs, was a guard. Bolivia froze in place. She waited for what seemed like an eternity, but the guard didn't budge, nor did he sleep.

Well, if she couldn't get back in her own tent, she'd do the next best thing. She'd sneak into Tooley's tent. He would surely admire the fact that she had evaded the guard just to pay him a midnight visit. From what she had discerned of his ego, he'd probably be flattered. Imagine instead of escaping when she had the opportunity, she had instead become overwhelmed with lust for him and crawled, in pain, to his tent. The guy would be knocked out by the story.

She backed up on her stomach to the rear of her tent, then wormed her way behind it until she was beside Tooley's. Then, very slowly and very cautiously, she inched around the other side of Tooley's tent and quietly unzipped the flap. She creeped inside and lay still in the darkness, getting up her nerve.

A flashlight came on, shining right in her face. She blinked as the circle of light blinded her.

"What a pleasant surprise," said Tooley. "A midnight visit from the fair Bolivia."

She couldn't help detecting the sarcasm and was afraid her little ploy wasn't going to work. Nevertheless, she tried to smile at him, but since the gag forced her to smile anyway, it probably wasn't discernible.

"I think this is the first time a woman has ever wanted to see me badly enough that she crawled all the way on her stomach," came the voice out of the darkness.

Was it worth it? Was it really worth it? She felt like she was selling her soul just to get the big story.

"Well, crawl over here, honey, and lets get cozy. If I had known this was going to occur I would have insisted on your showering today."

It *wasn't* worth it. This was perhaps the most humiliating moment of Bolivia's life.

"Of course, I knew you were attracted to me, coming back time and again to see me. Even I didn't expect you to crawl, though."

She could have killed him. She could have happily cut him up into little pieces and barbecued him.

"Oh, sweet thing, and you still have the gag in your mouth. It must be killing you not to be able to tell me yourself, in your own words, how you feel about me. Well, don't worry, honey, I know just how you feel. It's almost like an obsession, isn't it? I've felt that way once or twice in my life, too. Of course, I was just a kid then."

Death was too good for him. Slow torture. That was what she'd like to do to him. She'd like to tie him up and gag him and then degrade him just the way he was degrading her.

She heard a noise and then his lantern was turned on. She had been picturing him in bed for the night, but instead he was seated on his cot, fully dressed, his rifle lying across his knees. And he was smiling, of course. He always seemed to be smiling.

"Did you really think you were going to get away with it?" he asked her.

Thinking he was talking about her supposed seduction scene, she sat up with her back to him. There was no point in crawling out, but there was no point in giving him the satisfaction of facing him, either.

"We had you tracked from the moment you left your tent."

She turned back, feeling her eyes widen and not being able to control them.

"What happened? You made it to the path, why didn't you go on?"

Glad she had come back on her own rather than be dragged back, she hung her head.

"Chickened out, did you?"

She practically whirled around to face him.

Tooley laughed. "I figured that would get to you. But the fact is, you did chicken out. Was it the thought of appearing in Fort Lauderdale in your skivvies?"

Bolivia looked down. The T-shirt was twisted around her body and her white cotton panties were on view. Well, so what? They covered her better than any bathing suit she owned.

"What am I going to do with you, Bolivia?"

She crossed her legs, then motioned with her foot in the direction of the gag.

"Let you speak on your own behalf? No, I don't think so. I think it's more likely you would spit at me again."

Bolivia vigorously shook her head. Spitting was too good for him.

"I'm afraid I don't believe you."

All of a sudden the fight went out of her, and she hung her head in dejection. It wasn't worth it. None of it was worth it. More than anything else, she wanted to be back in Miami Beach in her hot apartment drinking a cold beer and complaining about the lack of air-conditioning.

She didn't see him move at first, but then he was standing over her. One hand reached down to ruffle the hair on her head, then stayed there. It was rather the way one treated a faithful dog. Just another humiliation, but Bolivia was too tired to summon up any anger.

Tooley knelt down in front of her and gently untied the gag. Then he pulled her head to his chest and kept it there. "Poor thing," he said, "don't take it so hard. I know you see yourself as a tough reporter, but you're really only a woman, aren't you?"

A tiny flicker of feeling began to flare.

"It's a losing proposition, sweetheart, and the sooner you realize it the better off you'll be."

The pig actually thought he'd broken her spirit.

"Well, you're being a good girl now, and I'm going to reward you. I'm going to untie you and let you sleep in my cot tonight, and in the morning everything is going to look better to you."

She leaned back from him, then got up on her knees so that they were eye-level. She summoned any dramatic ability she might possess in order to put a sweet, trusting look on her face, and in the instant she saw that she had succeeded, in the instant he changed his smile to one of benevolence, she thrust her head forward with all her strength into his nose and was rewarded with a satisfying crunch.

Tooley stood up with a bellow, blood gushing from his nose and already seeping into his red beard.

Shortly thereafter, a trussed and gagged Bolivia was dragged back to her tent. A trussed, gagged and idiotically happy Bolivia.

## Chapter 8

The sound of thunder woke her up shortly before daybreak, and the rain continued throughout the day. The tent didn't leak, but the ground beneath her began to get soaked. She thought tents were supposed to have bottoms to them but hers had nothing but bare ground beneath her.

She heard intermittent sounds outside her tent: men joking around, breakfast being served, the splashing of rain hitting the side of her tent.

She was feeling inertia as strong as a drug. She couldn't seem to form any plan, or even care very much about planning. She supposed what she had was a form of battle fatigue, or whatever it was prisoners got. She was sore all over; her ankles were throbbing, her throat was parched, and a headache had taken the place of hunger. She was also filthy and probably had insects living in her hair by this time. The idea of seducing Tooley now seemed a joke. She doubted whether she had the appeal left to seduce a vagrant.

It seemed as though they had forgotten her existence. Was she to just stay here, then, until she died of starvation? Did she even care? Was she feverish, or was it just the humidity that made her feel so exhausted?

She kept drifting in and out of a shallow sleep, so that when a voice spoke, she wasn't sure for a moment whether she was dreaming or awake.

"Bolivia? Can you hear me?"

She opened her eyes and glanced at the opening of the tent. Mason was looking in.

"Do I have permission to enter?"

She felt her eyes closing and her consciousness drifting away. She felt a hand on her forehead. Then she felt nothing for a while.

The movement hurt her, and she woke up to find she was being carried into Tooley's tent. They laid her down on his cot and then she felt her wrists being untied and the gag removed. She didn't feel any better with them off than she had with them on.

"This can't continue," Mason was saying.

"I wouldn't worry about her," said Tooley. "She's a tough one."

"She feels feverish, and she probably has an infection. I'm going to insist on giving her some antibiotics."

Her head was lifted and some water poured into her mouth. It was difficult, but she managed to swallow it without choking. Then she felt some pills being placed on her tongue, and she was given more water to wash them down.

"I want some hot water to wash her off with and some dry clothes," said Mason.

"She'll fight you like a wildcat if you try to change her clothes," said Tooley.

"She doesn't have it in her to fight anymore," said Mason.

Bolivia thought about that. This was beginning to sound very much like a death scene to her, and she wasn't anywhere near dying. Tired, yes; hungry, yes; but near death? Absolutely not.

She knew her body was being sponged off, her wounds tended to and the warmth of a blanket was drawn over her, but it seemed to be happening to someone else. She just wanted to sleep a little more, and then she'd be up to fighting again.

"Soup," she heard Mason say. "Chicken soup, and send out for it. I don't want it to take all day."

She summoned a little bit of energy that she didn't know she had and opened her eyes. Mason and Tooley were staring down at her, and both of them looked concerned.

"Hang in there," said Mason. "We're going to feed you some soup."

Bolivia's eyes shifted to Tooley.

"I'll feed you myself," said Tooley. "Mason here has been giving me hell for mistreating you. I'm sorry. I guess I figured you were tougher than you are."

A frisson of anger stirred within her. It wasn't enough to mount an all-out attack, but it was enough to scowl.

"Hey, you put up a good fight," said Tooley. "But come on, the odds were way against you."

She put all her effort into deepening the scowl.

"She just needs some tender, loving care," said Mason.

"Oh, indeed," said Tooley. "I'm even going to sing this little girl some lullabies after she's eaten."

She didn't know where it came from, but suddenly it was coming out. "I'm going on a hunger strike," said Bolivia, the words a mere whisper. She could tell they were heard, though, by the expression on their faces.

"Oh, no. No you're not," said Mason, sounding just like a mother. But Tooley was grinning and looking much more like his usual self.

"Don't worry," he said. "If she was planning on suicide, she wouldn't have swallowed the pills. Anyway, hunger strikes are only a means of getting publicity, and she's not in a position to get any."

Bolivia turned her head away from them. She would have liked to tell him to go to hell but she couldn't stay awake.

Suddenly there were several pillows being placed under her shoulders and head, and then Mason was pulling up a camp stool next to the cot. Somebody handed him a container of soup, and he stirred it around a little before bringing a spoonful to her mouth.

She looked around and saw Tooley at the other side of the tent, watching. He was wearing an olive green rain poncho, and water was dripping off it.

"No," she said to Mason, and then clamped her mouth shut.

"You're in a weakened condition," said Mason, "and I don't like it."

She didn't feel as if she were in a weakened condition. She suddenly felt in a position of power. If she refused to eat, wouldn't they have to let her go?

He put the spoon to her lips and let a little of the soup slide down her chin. In the next minute, he was wiping off her chin.

"We're going to have a few rules for prisoners put in effect around here," Mason told her. "You'll be guarded, but not tied up. You'll have three meals a day. You'll be allowed exercise periods. And one of the guys even bought you some magazines to read while he was out getting your soup. Tooley let this go much too far, although I have to say you're partly to blame."

"I don't know," said Tooley. "Untied, exercise, plenty of food, what makes you think she won't escape? I say, let her starve to death."

She realized that now he was trying to get her to eat just to spite him.

"What do you say?" asked Mason.

"No," said Bolivia, and then she was drifting off again.

At first she thought it was a dream, the voice coming out of the darkness. Then she realized it couldn't be a dream or it wouldn't feel so good to be able to lie on her back without her arms being tied behind her.

She heard Tooley say, "You remind me of my kid sister. She was always a pest, always following after me, always wanting me to show her how to do everything. Always wanting to be just like me. Not that you want to be just like me—it's obvious you don't—but you've both got the same kind of nose trouble, always poking your noses in where they don't belong."

His voice sounded different. He wasn't being bossy now, or flirtatious, or any of the other ways she'd heard him sound. It was more as if he were talking to himself, reminiscing. She didn't mind listening to him—it was soothing.

"Her name is Anne, but I always called her Antsy. She's married now, has a bunch of kids of her own. I haven't seen her in over two years, and the last time was just for a few minutes when I had to change planes in Dallas and she drove in to see me."

Antsy. Bolivia thought of Annie. Annie and her wedding and her bridesmaids' dresses. She wondered if Annie would end up with a bunch of kids, but she didn't think so.

Workaholics usually didn't take the time off to have kids. She could see Jack with kids, though; maybe he'd talk her into it.

"There was this one time, Antsy got up on the garage roof with an umbrella and announced she could fly. Well, she flew all right, straight down to the ground and broke her arm in three places. And I got the blame for it. I hadn't done it with an umbrella, though. I'd made myself a hang glider. Only trouble was, it could hang but it couldn't glide. I didn't hurt anything but my pride, though, but then, I was big even then."

Bolivia had taken flying lessons once. She'd figured if she couldn't make it as a foreign correspondent, maybe she'd make it as a bush pilot. She never did it much anymore, though, because it cost too much to rent a plane.

"You're not going to believe this, but I wrote poetry when I was a kid. I didn't call it poetry, of course. I called it lyrics to rock songs. But it was poetry. Thing is, other kids, they hear you're writing poetry, they all of a sudden start to avoid you. But everyone admired rock songs. Mostly about girls. That was the period when I was starting to like girls, only I didn't know how to get along with them because the only girl I knew real well was my sister, and all we ever did was fight.

"There was this one girl, Jannine, I had this humongous crush on, must have been about fifteen at the time. She was a real barracuda, went through boys on an average of one a week. Pretty, of course. She couldn't have gotten away with it if she wasn't pretty. I was six feet already, too clumsy to play basketball, but I was on the junior varsity football team. I thought I was hot stuff when Jannine started giving me the eye in the hall one day, and I got up my nerve and called her up and asked her out for the next Saturday night. My dad drove me over to pick her up, and she came out of the house, took one look at my father in the driver's seat and told me she thought I was older. Told me she didn't date boys who didn't have their driver's licenses yet.

"I think I must have written fifteen poems just about Jannine."

Bolivia felt warm and then cool, sometimes both at once. The voice coming out of the darkness was comforting, rather like being wrapped up in someone's arms. She didn't understand what he was talking about, but the words didn't matter. It was the background noise she liked.

"Some of the men are calling me a sadist, or worse. Of course, some of them are saying I ought to whip you, but they're not the ones I usually listen to. I never meant to hurt you physically. Mentally, yes, I was hoping to break your spirit. Not totally break it, you understand, but just bend it to my will.

"What I didn't take into consideration was the humidity. I mean, you seemed tough, I figured your ankles and wrists were tough ... well, maybe I wasn't thinking. I just didn't think about infections. Yeah, I heard you get a cut in Florida, it's open to infection, but it never happened to me and ... Hell, I'm not making excuses. I'm not trying to justify anything. I'm responsible for your condition, and I screwed up, that's all. We'll take better care of you after this.

"But why'd you have to come back? I figured the last time you were here you got the message. I guess it was the first time. I guess I enjoyed talking to you too much, and it must've showed. Well, not talking so much as arguing, I guess.

"There's something about you that gets to me—it did from the start. It's not that I want to break you, I swear. It's just that—damn it, you drive me nuts with that smart mouth of yours. Sorry, I didn't mean to yell. I don't even know if you can hear me, anyway. Those big, brown eyes of yours, they drive me nuts, too. I don't think I've ever seen eyes that big. They can look so hurt and so mad at the same time. But it's that mouth that gets to me. I gotta admit it, it was a pleasure to gag it. Drove you crazy not to be able to talk back to me, didn't it? Yeah, I know it did. It would drive *me* nuts. Can you hear me? Do you understand what I'm saying? Bolivia?"

It was dark when she woke up, but she was feeling better. That had been the first good sleep she'd had, and the antibiotics must also have helped. She was hungry, sure, but she was still a long way from even approaching starvation.

She reached down to the side of the cot and found a canteen that Mason had no doubt left there. She unscrewed the cap and drank about half of the contents, then put it back where she had found it. She felt around some more to see if she could come up with Tooley's flashlight, but he must have moved it.

She sat up and swung her legs over the side of the bed, wrapping the blanket around her. If the foot locker was still in here, she could put on some of Tooley's clothes and maybe make a break for it. She wouldn't take a path this time; she'd just head straight into the jungle and hope she came out in civilization.

She was just standing up when the tent flap opened and Tooley came in, holding a lantern.

"Going somewhere?" he asked her, but his tone wasn't as sarcastic as usual.

"It's too warm under the blanket. I was hoping to find some clothes." She kept her voice reasonable, not ready yet to start another fight with him.

He put down the lantern and opened his footlocker. He tossed her a pair of white boxer shorts and a black T-shirt, then turned his back while she got into them. The soft cotton felt wonderful after the scratchy blanket.

"You decent?" he asked her.

"I'm dressed, if that's what you mean."

He closed the lid of the footlocker and sat down on it. "Can I get you anything else?"

She shook her head.

"You're looking better."

"I'm not dead yet, Tooley."

"I can see that." He looked down at his hands for a moment, avoiding her eyes. "We collected a lot of rainwater today. What I was wondering is, would you want to wash your hair?"

She looked at the bandages around her wrists and ankles. It seemed a great deal of trouble when they'd all have to be done over again if she got them wet.

"I don't mean in the shower," said Tooley. "I could bring a basin of water in here. In fact, I could wash it for you."

Her head came up, alert. This offer didn't sound in character for Tooley at all. She could tell him to go to hell, which was her first thought, but on second thought, why not get some clean hair out of it? As it was, her head was itching like crazy. And it wouldn't be giving in, because it was a hunger strike she was on not a hair-wash strike. And it just might do something for her morale to see him in a subservient position.

"Okay," said Bolivia.

"Okay what? You want to wash it?"

"Okay, I want *you* to wash it."

Tooley looked as though he'd like to give her an argument, but since it had been his suggestion he couldn't very well. He left the tent, and when he came back, he was carrying a basin of water. He went out again and returned with two more water-filled buckets.

He got a bottle of shampoo out of the footlocker, then set the basin on top of it and asked her to sit in front of it and lean her head back.

The few steps over to the footlocker were painful, and Bolivia realized just how out of shape she was. Exercise was going to be a priority.

She leaned back her head as far as it would go, and Tooley began to splash water over her hair.

"Better close your eyes," he said. "I'll probably get soap in them."

The angle of her head was making her neck sore, but no more so than the rest of her body. And then he was rubbing shampoo into her hair, and it felt wonderful. A moment later his fingers were busy massaging her scalp.

"Feel good?" asked Tooley.

Bolivia shrugged.

"You know damn well it does, but you're too stubborn to admit it."

She was sorry when the massaging part ended and he started rinsing her hair with the buckets of water. At the end he handed her a towel, and she wrapped it around her head and went back to sitting on the cot.

"How come you wear your hair so short?" he asked her.

"How come you wear yours so long?"

"I like it long."

"Well, I like mine short. I don't even have to comb it that way."

Tooley paused in handing her his comb and put it back in his pocket. She started rubbing her hair with the towel until it was halfway dry, and then she ran her fingers through it. She couldn't believe she was so spoiled by civilization that a clean head of hair meant so much to her. If she wanted to be a war correspondent she'd better forget about that kind of stuff.

"I could rustle us up some coffee if you're interested," Tooley offered.

Bolivia shook her head.

"No nutritional value in coffee, as far as I know," said Tooley. "Hunger strikes don't usually include beverages."

"Yes they do," said Bolivia.

"Hey, Tooley, you in there?" came a voice from outside the tent.

"Bring it in, Bobby Joe," said Tooley.

Bobby Joe entered carrying a second cot, which he set up on the other side of the tent. "Hi, Bolivia," he said to her.

"Hi, Bobby Joe."

"How about a cup of tea?" he asked her.

"Thanks."

Tooley shook his head. "You'll take a cup of tea from him, but not a cup of coffee from me."

"No nutritional value in tea that I know of," said Bolivia.

"Don't be so sure. Bobby Joe drinks herbal tea."

*Betrayed*

"Lemon Zinger," said Bobby Joe, winking at her as he left the tent.

"Why's there another cot in here?" asked Bolivia.

"So you don't have to sleep on the ground."

"Why can't I be in here alone?"

"Bolivia, you're not exactly a guest here. Anyway, it'll make for double guards. I know that plans of escape are already forming in that devious mind of yours."

"Prisoners of war are obligated to try to escape," she said.

"You're not a prisoner of war. You're just a nosy reporter who saw too much, so don't go puffing yourself up."

"In contrast to you, a Vietnam vet, who now fancies himself some kind of soldier of war?"

"Is that what you think?"

Bolivia shrugged.

"You got something against Vietnam vets?"

Bolivia looked away.

"What were you, one of those antiwar demonstrators?"

"I was just a kid," she said.

Tooley stood up. "I know what you think of me, Bolivia. A little less educated than you. A little less socially aware because in order to be socially aware you have to be social to begin with. The kind of person who couldn't get a college deferment and didn't have the savvy to burn his draft card, the bucks to go to Sweden or the intelligence to go to Canada. So I ended up in Southeast Asia with all the other suckers. And if there hadn't been a war on, I'd probably be the guy servicing your car today."

Bolivia shook her head. "No. You're the type who can't wait for a war. You're the type who'd start one just to have something to do."

"Is that how you see me?"

"Genghis Khan come to life."

He started for the opening to the tent, then seemed to change his mind and sat back down.

"What time is it?" she asked.

"Late."

"Where's my watch?"

"Safe. It's with your wallet and key chain. They'll be returned to you when you leave."

"How are you going to let me leave here alive, Tooley? Have you thought about that?"

"I've thought about it."

Bobby Joe came in carrying a mug of coffee for Tooley and a mug of tea for Bolivia. He handed it to her and said, "Can I get you anything else?"

"No thanks, Bobby Joe," she said.

"A sandwich? Maybe some crackers?"

She shook her head.

With his back blocking Tooley's view, he slipped a candy bar out of his pocket and held it out to her. Then he winked. Bolivia took it from him and hid it under the blanket. She wasn't above cheating if she could get away with it.

"See you guys later," said Booby Joe, going out of the tent and zipping up the flap.

She sipped at the tea, but it wasn't satisfying. Not now that she knew there was a Mounds bar hidden under the blanket. But how she was going to get the wrapper off without Tooley hearing, she didn't know.

"If you got some crazy idea that we're going to kill you," said Tooley, "forget it. If we were the kind of guys who did things like that, we would've killed you already."

*Betrayed*

"I just don't see how you're going to let me go. As soon as you do, I'll write the story. I'll also have you arrested." But before that, I'll eat a candy bar, if I can figure out how to get rid of you long enough.

"All we're going to need is enough time to clear out of here before you call the cops."

"That's not much time."

"I know."

"I can get to the cops pretty fast. One of my best friends is on the force."

"That compounds the problem, doesn't it?"

"What day is it?"

"Early Thursday morning."

"People know where I am, Tooley. I'm surprised no one's come after me yet." She'd never wanted anything as much in her life as she wanted that Mounds bar.

"All we need is another forty-eight hours."

"And then what? You magically disappear?"

"Something like that." Tooley got up and came over to her cot, sitting down beside her. All she could think about was that he was sitting on her candy bar, until he pulled her over and put his arm around her.

"What do you think you're doing?" she asked him, shoving his arm away.

"Hey, we weren't fighting, were we? We were actually getting along for a few minutes there." He put both arms around her this time, and instead of pushing him away, she stiffened her body.

"I'm not feeling very friendly toward you, Tooley," she said between clenched teeth.

"Relax, I'm not going to hurt you. You just looked so pitiful all of a sudden, your hair sticking out every which way, your skinny legs hanging out of my baggy shorts, those big eyes like a frightened little kid. I'm sorry about what I've done to you, Bolivia, I really am."

She felt herself relax a little and leaned into his chest. The attraction was still there, and her defenses appeared to be momentarily down. What would it hurt to take a little comfort from him?

"That's better," he said, his lips going to the top of her head and nuzzling her hair. She felt like running her hands through the furry pelt of his forearm, then up to feel his smooth biceps. She found him a hell of a sexy man, even when she was spitting at him. Maybe especially when she was spitting at him.

"What would you be doing if you weren't here?" he asked her.

She moved her head back and forth a little across his chest. "Probably having a beer, looking out over the ocean, getting ready to go to bed."

"Well, I don't have an ocean, but I could find us some beers."

She shook her head. "Unlike coffee and tea, beer does have nutritional value."

"Forget about that hunger strike. It's a lot of nonsense."

"I'll forget about it as soon as you give me my things and let me go."

She felt his muscles flex and then slowly relax again. "Okay, no beer, and I don't have an ocean for you, but we could always go to bed."

She lifted her head up, not in answer to what he was suggesting, but because she wanted to see his face. It was serious for once, and at the moment when she met his eyes, his mouth closed over hers. It was still very sore in the corners from the gag, but his lips were gentle, and his beard tickled in a pleasurable way. She reached up one hand to feel his springy, red curls, then tugged at his hair, trying to tell him that he didn't have to be so gentle with her.

He was already pulling her over his lap as he shoved the blanket to one side, and then something flew onto the floor and landed with a slight thud.

Tooley looked down, then let go of her as he reached for the candy bar.

"What do we have here?" he asked, looking from the candy bar to her.

"I never saw it before," said Bolivia, moving away from him on the cot.

"A Mounds bar. Now that would be Bobby Joe, I'd say. He's always got one sticking out of his pocket."

"He must have dropped it while he was in here," said Bolivia, wondering if she could knock him out and grab the candy. Her lust for Tooley was nothing compared to her lust for that chocolate bar.

"Or he might have slipped it to you when I wasn't looking."

"I don't know anything about it, Tooley. I happen to be on a hunger strike."

He gave her a careful look. "Of course. That pure slipped my mind. And here I was thinking that you had it hidden to eat when you got a chance. Forgive me, Bolivia."

She watched with alarm as he began to rip the wrapper off one end of the candy bar. And then he was pulling out half of it and taking a bite.

"Ummm, not bad," he said. "Not my favorite kind, but it hits the spot." He smiled at her, showing chocolate teeth. "Want a bite?"

She shook her head, almost overcome by the smell of the chocolate and coconut.

He made a great production out of smacking his lips, then bit into it again. "Sure you don't want a bite, sweetie?"

"Go to hell," she said, getting up off the cot and walking across the tent. She lay down on the other cot and turned her back to him. Maybe it wouldn't hurt so much if she didn't see him eating it.

"No more snuggling, Bolivia? And just when we were getting so cozy."

She couldn't believe she had actually allowed that monster to touch her. To kiss her. She must have a fever, because she sure didn't have any other explanation.

"If we kissed right now, you'd be able to taste it," he said, almost chuckling on the words.

She could picture him with chocolate in the corners of his mouth, and the picture was nauseating. She should never have let her guard down for a moment. She shouldn't have let him even sit on her cot. If she hadn't, the candy bar would still be in her possession.

She heard the chuckle then, out in the open. "The problem is, Bolivia, you still think you're smarter than I am. You think you can put one over on me. Sorry, babe, but that just ain't the way it is."

Oh, God, he sounded smug. But she had just the thing to demolish him.

"Hey, Tooley," she said. "Guess what?"

"What?"

"I know about Tamoros."

## Chapter 9

Bolivia rolled over on the cot to see Tooley's expression as he leaped up and landed halfway across the tent. Revenge was sweet, she thought, seeing the stunned look on his face turn to incredulity and then anger. Even sweeter than the candy bar he had dropped and was now stepping on in his haste to get to her.

His hands were reaching for her throat, but he stopped short of strangling her and dropped his arms to his sides. He seemed to regain his composure as he said, "I don't know what you're talking about."

"Right," said Bolivia. "That's why you were instantly at my throat."

"I hope for your sake that you didn't say what I think you said, because if you did, that makes your situation much more serious."

"Do I get the firing squad?" asked Bolivia, hardly even interested in the candy bar that was now stuck to the bottom of his boot.

He flung his head back and seemed to be staring at the top of the tent. In that position his red hair hung halfway down his back, but instead of giving him the appearance of a rock star, he looked like a Viking warrior. She could very easily picture him with horns on his head and a sword at his waist.

When he looked back down at her, his look was measuring. "What do you know about Tamoros?"

"Caribbean island, formerly belonged to—"

"Don't play games with me!"

"You asked me what I knew."

"You know what I want. What do you know about Tamoros in the context of your being here."

"Maybe if you asked me nicely, Tooley..."

He was suddenly standing over her, his eyes threatening. She smiled. It hurt the corners of her mouth, but she didn't care.

"Don't you understand?" he asked. "I'm only trying to protect you."

"Tell me another one."

"I know it may seem hard to believe—"

"Try *impossible*," said Bolivia. "The only one I seem to need protection from around here is you."

"Anything I've done has been for your own good."

She looked rather pointedly at the bandages around her wrists.

Some light in Tooley seemed to be extinguished. His shoulders slumped, his body visibly relaxed, and he walked over to his footlocker and lifted the lid. She was expecting him to remove something important, but all he took out was a cotton scarf, which he then proceeded to tie around his hair, fashioning it into a ponytail. Then he took out two apples and tossed her one. The other one he bit into.

She ignored the apple, wondering what he was up to now.

"Go on, eat it," said Tooley. "It's not poisoned. And I'm not trying to get anything out of you in exchange, either."

He sounded defeated, or maybe at peace. At any rate, he wasn't the same combatant of a moment before.

Nevertheless, Bolivia ignored the apple. This wasn't the Garden of Eden, and innocence had dropped by the wayside long ago.

"You rode a motorcycle here?" asked Tooley.

Bolivia nodded.

"Want to run away with me?"

"Sure, Tooley, just what I've been dying for."

"I mean it. You and me, why don't we cut out of here?"

Bolivia sat up on the cot and picked up the apple. Whatever he was up to, she was already tired of her hunger strike. Anyway, she would have exchanged innocence and just about anything else at the moment in order to bite into the apple.

"I'm serious," he said, not even gloating over the fact that she had just accepted his bribe. "This isn't worth it, none of it. Tying you up, keeping you prisoner, it's nonsense. But I'm not about to let you go then stick around for the consequences. Ever had a yen to see Mexico? We could ride down there, maybe get to know each other."

"Do you have a split personality, or have I missed something?" Bolivia asked.

He gave her an apologetic smile. "I don't even want to hear what you know. Let's just get the hell out of here and sort it out later."

"Is this good cop/bad cop with you playing both parts?"

He shook his head and started to open his mouth, then shut it again, as though knowing no words were going to convince her.

He reached into his foot locker, bringing out a pair of socks. He knelt down on the floor in front of her, then slowly, gently, removed Bobby Joe's now-muddy socks, pulling the clean socks on her feet and up over the bandages.

He got a clean shirt and a pair of pants and tossed them to her. "Put them on," he said, but it was said in a casual way, not like an order.

Bolivia set down the apple core and got dressed. What the hell, she felt more in control with some clothes on. She was starting to roll up the pants legs when Tooley knelt down again, this time with a knife in his hands, and cut off the pants so that they were the right length. He buttoned the cuffs of the long shirt, then turned them back a couple of times. They were still long enough to cover the bandages, but not long enough to impede her fingers.

She was holding up the pants with one hand, and he brought out a length of rope to use as a belt. The final touch was the helmet he placed on her head.

"You look just like a guy," he said. "I'd give you back your boots, but I don't want them rubbing against your ankles." Then he handed her her wallet and keys.

"You're letting me escape?" she asked him.

"Hell no, I'm going with you." He put his hands on her shoulders and pulled her to him. When his arms went around her, she let her own hang down, wondering what in the world he was up to.

"You don't trust me," he said.

"Why the hell should I?"

He took her hand. "Come on, we're getting out of here."

"Why?"

"I don't like what's happening to you."

"You're *responsible* for what's happened to me."

"I know it looks that way—"

"It *is* that way."

"Quit giving me a hard time and take advantage of the fact that I just had a change of conscience and I'm getting you out of here."

"Change of *conscience*? You mean you have a conscience?"

"You're an innocent bystander, and this has all been my fault. If I hadn't flirted with you the first time you came here, you never would've come back."

Bolivia took a step away, pulling her hand out of his. "I came back for a story, not because you flirted with me."

"I'm trying to be honest, why can't you?"

What the hell, what did it matter? "The third time, maybe," she said, "but the second time I was still looking for a story."

"I think we could get along—"

"As long as you keep me gagged!"

"We'll take turns, okay? Sometimes you can gag me."

They both heard the sound of the flap being unzipped at the same moment. Bolivia sat back down on the cot and watched the expression in Tooley's eyes turn to panic.

Mason poked his head in. "I want to give Bolivia some more antibiotics before I turn in," he said, then came into the tent.

His eyes went to Bolivia for the first time. "What's this?" he asked. "You taking her on a night march, Tooley?"

For the first time in her experience, Tooley seemed at a loss for words. "No, he's taking me on the invasion," said Bolivia.

Tooley froze in place. "I beg your pardon?" said Mason, giving Bolivia an innocent look.

"I'm going along on the invasion of Tamoros," she said.

"You have permission for this?" Mason asked Tooley.

It was the first occasion Bolivia had heard that Tooley wasn't the one in charge.

"She's talking—" Tooley started to say, but Bolivia cut him off with, "I'll look like just another Tamoron." She stood and turned around for Mason's inspection. "Don't you think I could pass for a man?"

"A pretty boy, I guess," said Mason. "But you're still a woman, and I don't approve of women in combat."

"Remind me to challenge you to some wrestling when my wrists have healed," said Bolivia.

Mason started to smile. "Remind me to find out how you ever talked Tooley into this."

Tooley opened his mouth to speak, and Bolivia said, "I'll take those pills if you have them."

"Oh, sure," said Mason, reaching into his pocket and bringing out a bottle. He handed it to her. "Take two of the white ones every four hours until they're gone. Of course, we'll probably be gone by then, too. I put in a couple of sleeping pills, too, in case you need them. They're the blue ones."

"And Mason," said Bolivia.

"Yes?"

*Betrayed* 145

"Do you think you could scrounge me up something to eat?"

"It'll probably be junk food at this hour, but I'll see what I can do."

"That's okay," said Bolivia. "I love junk food."

Tooley followed Mason out, as though hoping she'd escape in his absence. Well, she wasn't going anywhere—except Tamoros, of course. She didn't have any idea what had brought on his change of heart, but she was more determined than ever. It wasn't likely she'd ever again walk into a situation that could so quickly and decisively further her career.

She was doing some stretching exercises when the flap opened again. Mason had beaten Tooley back and was carrying some clothes in addition to a couple of canned soft drinks and assorted bags of potato chips and the like.

Mason, who was only about half an inch shorter than her, said, "I have a feeling my clothes will be a better fit than Tooley's. If you want them, that is."

"Thanks," she said, taking them out of his arms.

"You know," he said, "this isn't such a bad idea. Normally I'd say that a woman would only cause dissension, but the feeling around camp has been just about a hundred percent in your favor. Tooley's popularity has gone way down since his treatment of you."

"It was just a little test of wills," said Bolivia, deciding she could afford to be magnanimous, since she had won.

"Well, if you want anything else, you just let me know. And I'm real glad to see you up and looking better."

Bolivia had gone through an orange soda and a bag of pretzels and was on a cold Doctor Pepper and some fig bars when Tooley came back. He was smoking a cigar and didn't even ask if the smoke bothered her. She guessed the truce was at an end.

He lay down on the other cot and faced the ceiling. "How the hell did you ever find out about the invasion?"

"It was just deduction," said Bolivia, talking with her mouth full. "Reporters are good at deduction."

He muttered something that made her laugh. "Deduction hell!" he said. "I want to know how you found out."

"I overheard it."

"You couldn't have overheard it."

"It was the night I was escaping. That's why I came back. I heard some of the Tamorons talking in one of the tents."

"They don't speak English."

Bolivia kept chewing.

"I said—"

"I speak Spanish."

He was silent for a moment. "Fluently?"

"Pretty much."

"Enough to pass for a Tamoron?"

Bolivia shrugged. She thought the problem was going to be passing for a man, not a Tamoron.

"It's not too late for us to leave."

"I don't want to leave," said Bolivia.

"If we are invading Tamoros—and I'm not saying we are—you could be killed."

Bolivia shrugged.

"I said—"

"I heard what you said. I could also wind up with the biggest story of my career. And an exclusive, at that."

"Is that all you care about?"

"Yes."

"You'd risk your life for a story?"

"Hell, yes. At least I'm risking my life *for* something."

"What's that supposed to mean?"

"What are you? Some soldier of fortune hired by the government? You're just risking your life for money. Or is it the thrill?"

He seemed to be about to speak, then clamped his mouth shut.

"Or are you government?" she asked. "CIA, by chance?"

"You one of those reporters who don't trust the CIA?" he asked.

Bolivia smiled.

"Well?"

"No reporter trusts the CIA," she said.

"I think you have the wrong idea," said Tooley.

"I don't think so."

"I think you think I'm in charge of this."

"You seem to be the one giving the orders."

"I'm only in charge of a small part of the operation. Mostly we're just training some of the Tamorons in combat."

"Are you going to train me in combat?" Bolivia asked him.

"Forget it!"

"I'm pretty good with a rifle already."

"Would you be interested in striking a deal?"

"Let's hear it."

"We'll put you up in a hotel, with a guard, and if the invasion's a success, you'll be flown over, at government expense, and given exclusive interviews with the new political leaders. You wouldn't be in the hotel more than twenty-four hours. You can stay here until the invasion and talk to some of the Tamorons, if you want."

"Sorry," said Bolivia.

"How can you turn down an offer like that? Any reporter in the world would jump at it."

"It's more than a story," said Bolivia. "If I'm actually part of the invasion, I can get a book out of it."

"Not greedy or anything, are you?"

"And probably a foreign assignment."

"Would you believe me if I told you it's your life I'm worried about?"

"No."

"I wasn't kidding before, about running off to Mexico together."

"I think you were just getting cold feet."

"Come again?"

"I think you were chickening out. I think it was your life you were worried about."

"You asking for a gag again?"

"Is that your first response when someone disagrees with you, Tooley?"

He snorted. "With you it seems to be."

She set down her soda on the floor and stood. "Tooley?"

"What?"

"I have to go to the bathroom."

"Use one of the buckets."

"I don't want to use a bucket. I want to go in the jungle."

"You're not going to get any privacy during the invasion."

"I'll hold it during the invasion."

He waved an arm. "Go on, why don't you escape while you're at it?"

"You wish," she said, as she unzipped the tent flap.

Tooley was pretending to be asleep when she got back to the tent, but he didn't fool her. Instead of being relaxed in sleep his face was set almost in a grimace, which meant, no doubt, that he was thinking of her.

She stripped down to the boxer shorts and T-shirt, but left her socks on. Then she washed down one of the blue pills with the last of her soft drink.

The pillows were all on Tooley's cot, so she went over and pulled one from under his head. His eyes opened. "Turn the lantern out while you're at it," he said.

"No final arguments?" she asked him.

"I'm past arguing with you."

That made her laugh.

"At least for tonight," he said.

The sleeping pill seemed to kick in almost immediately. She could feel herself drifting to sleep, the soreness in her body forgotten.

"Just one thing," came Tooley's voice out of the darkness.

"Umm," she said.

"If you already knew about the invasion, how come you didn't mention it?"

"I didn't feel like I could confide in you."

"You would've saved yourself a lot of pain."

"I can take pain."

Tooley grunted.

"I'm tougher than you think, Tooley."

"I think I know how tough you are by this time."

"But not tough enough to go along on an invasion?"

"Go to sleep, Bolivia."

"That's what I was trying to do." She rolled over on her side and hung one foot off the cot. She heard a noise but it came to her faintly, through layers of consciousness. Then she felt a blanket being drawn over her and then a hand pushing the hair out of her face. It felt like when she was sick as a child and her mother had comforted her. Bolivia made a little humming noise of pleasure and felt the hand leave. Wrapped in a warm cocoon, she fell deeply into sleep.

*She was racing down I-95 on her motorcycle, and she was late. She was late for the wedding, she was dressed wrong, and Annie was going to kill her.*

*Everything was taking ten times longer than usual; the turnoffs didn't come when they were supposed to; the ride to Coral Gables, which usually took fifteen minutes, was stretching past an hour; and no matter that she was breaking the speed limit, her cycle seemed to be coasting.*

*An eternity later she arrived at Jack's house. Wedding guests had lined their cars on both sides of the street, and she had to pull her motorcycle up on Jack's front lawn in order to get a place.*

*She ran to the front door and opened it, knowing that the wedding must have started, that surely Annie wasn't still waiting for her arrival in order to begin. Instead of the entry hall she remembered, the door opened onto an enormous space the size of a ballroom. Hundreds of people were lined up on either side of an aisle, and they all turned their heads at her entrance.*

*At the end of the aisle she saw Annie in her wedding dress. Instead of the cream color she had described, the dress was shocking pink, with layers of ruffles that cascaded down the back and formed a train of several feet. Beside Annie, dressed in black with a black veil covering her face, was the diminutive form of Sandy.*

# Betrayed

*Walking as softly as possible so as not to be heard on the marble floor, Bolivia could still hear the thudding sound her boots were making as she plodded forward to join the wedding party. Her boots were covered with mud; her khakis dirty and stained with blood; and she had forgotten to remove her motorcycle helmet.*

*She marched forward in long strides but seemed to get no closer to the bride and groom. Her eyes forward, to avoid the stares of the crowd, she noticed that Jack's short, black hair was now fashioned into a red ponytail. Her eyes moved to the man beside him, surely his best man, and again she saw a red ponytail.*

*She thought it was funny and tried not to smile. But why would anyone be playing a joke at something as serious as a wedding?*

*For the first time the music penetrated her mind. A Sousa march was being played, her legs moving in time to the cadence. She looked around to see if anyone else saw the disparity between the music and the ceremony, and she saw that every man in the crowd was wearing his long, red hair in a ponytail. And every woman was dressed in black with a black veil.*

*Suddenly there was the sound of gunfire, and Bolivia threw herself to the floor and covered her head. When the sound of shots didn't stop and no screams ensued, she raised her head and saw all the men pointing their rifles at the ceiling in some kind of salute.*

*Bolivia got to her feet and continued her march. She quickened the pace, marching now to the rhythm of the shots, almost trotting in her haste to get to the head of the aisle and not be too late for the ceremony.*

*At last she arrived and saw Annie's welcoming smile. She felt relief that she wasn't in trouble after all, and she turned to smile at Jack.*

*Instead of Jack, though, the groom was Tooley, and he was grinning at her in consternation. "But you can't marry him," Bolivia started to say, and then Tooley was ripping off his bow tie and in the next second he was gagging her with it.*

*"Noooooo," she screamed, but no one heard her.*

# Chapter 10

Mason unwrapped the bandages from her wrists and nodded his approval. "You heal quickly. Leave them off and let the air get to them." She wondered if she'd end up with scars around her wrists. She wouldn't mind them, wouldn't mind being able to show them to people and say, "This is from the time I was kept prisoner and tied up." As a reporter, being kept prisoner had a certain cachet.

Her ankles were also healing, but he wrapped them in gauze again and gave her a pair of his boots and a couple of pairs of socks for padding. He applied some petroleum jelly to the corners of her mouth and told her not to eat it off.

Before Tooley returned Mason said, "Are you sure you know what you're getting into?"

Feeling the sympathy coming from him she said, "Why, have you changed your mind about helping me escape?"

"No. I just wonder if you know what you're doing."

"Look," said Bolivia, "I happen to agree with what you're doing. I have friends who are Tamorons, and I'd like to see them be able to return to their country."

He gave her a dubious look.

"Well, okay, not exactly friends, but I've seen where they live, and I feel sorry for them. And I sure don't like what's happening to Tamoros."

"Umm," said Mason, the sound as noncommittal a noise as she had ever heard.

"It's history being made, Mason. I want to be part of it."

"A war is no place for women."

Bolivia grinned. "But it's a great place for a reporter. And maybe I look like nothing more than a woman to you, but I'm a reporter first and foremost."

A cheer went up from the men when Bolivia swaggered out to join them for breakfast. Dressed in Mason's clothes, a helmet on her head and a gun belt hanging from her hips, she was feeling like one of the guys. Room was made for her at one of the tables, and she chatted with them in English and Spanish as she ate.

They were still sitting over coffee when Tooley showed up and shouted an order. The men all left the tables and double-marched to the center of the clearing, where they lined up in formation. Bolivia started to join them, but Tooley stopped her with a wave of his arm.

"You can help clean up," he told her.

Bolivia marched over to him. "I want to train with the guys, not be stuck with KP duty."

"Just do as you're told."

"I'm not one of your soldiers to order around."

## Betrayed

Tooley's eyes swept from her helmet to her boots. "You could've fooled me."

"Go to hell!"

"You'll follow orders like everyone else."

"And if I don't?"

"It's not too late to be gagged again, you know."

"I already know how to do dishes, but I don't know anything about the invasion."

"And you're not going to."

"Then how am I supposed to help?"

Tooley grabbed her arm and tried to walk her back to the tables, but she resisted and stood firm.

"Bolivia, you're not going to be issued a weapon, and you're not going to be part of the invasion."

"Like hell I'm not!"

"You're a reporter. You want a story, you'll get a story. I can even promise you an exclusive. But reporters who go to the front lines don't take part in the fighting."

"But I want to."

"I thought what you wanted was a story?"

"I do. But it would be an even better story if I could say I was a part of it."

"Write whatever you want, but in reality you're going to be well behind the lines."

"Are you telling me to lie?"

"I thought reporters did it all the time."

"Well, I'm not doing dishes."

"Fine, do push-ups then, but just stay out of our way."

Bolivia did push-ups; she did sit-ups. She did stretching exercises and jogged around the clearing. In the distance she could hear rifle fire, and not for the first time she felt as if she were being left out of real life because she was female.

Henry didn't take her seriously when she said she wanted to be in the middle of the action; her friends didn't take her seriously when she said she wouldn't mind living in Beirut; now Tooley wasn't taking her seriously when she said she wanted in on the invasion. The only person who had taken her seriously was her mother. Bolivia was six when the boys in the neighborhood had refused to allow her in their football game. She had told her mother then that she'd rather have been born a boy. "We all would," her mother had told her, "but those are the breaks." After that Bolivia had started to make the breaks for herself.

The guys came back for lunch, and after lunch they all headed for their tents. Siesta time. Bolivia didn't feel like a siesta; she felt like playing war games.

She watched Tooley head for the orange tent. When he got there he looked back at her. "Rest time," he called out to her.

She followed him inside but only to give him an argument. "I don't feel like resting," she told him. "All I've been doing since I got here is resting."

"That was enforced rest."

"What do you call this?" she asked, sitting down on her cot.

"Well, maybe you don't need a rest, but I do."

"I'm not tired."

"Read those magazines Bobby Joe brought you."

"I don't read fashion magazines."

Tooley chuckled. "Maybe you ought to give them a try."

"What's that supposed to mean?"

"Obviously you haven't looked in a mirror lately."

Bolivia got up from the cot and kicked the fashion magazines across the tent. She had a feeling that if there were a mirror handy, she would like what she saw. She'd always liked the way she looked in a motorcycle helmet, and this one wasn't much different.

She said, "I wish I had some paper and a pen."

"What for?"

"I'm a writer. I could get a head start on my story if I had something to write with."

"Would that make you happy?"

"It would help."

Tooley got a notebook and a pen out of his footlocker and handed them to her. "Now play quietly while I get some sleep, okay?" He went back to his cot and stretched out with his hands clasped beneath his head.

"What're you doing with paper and a pen?"

"Maybe I write letters home to my wife."

That shut her up fast. A wife? Tooley married? Was it conceivable? "You couldn't have a wife," she said, although she wasn't all that sure of it.

"Why not?"

"Who'd have you?"

Tooley said, "I'd love to argue my good qualities with you, but I need to get some sleep."

"Aren't you a little old for naps?"

"I haven't been getting much sleep lately for some damn reason. I can't imagine why."

Tooley shut his eyes, and she allowed him about ten seconds of rest before she said, "Are you really married?"

One eye opened. "Does it matter?"

"Not to me," said Bolivia, a little too quickly.

"Good," he said, and the eye closed as he rolled over so that his back was to her.

The spark of anger, already touched off, flared and she couldn't control it. She picked up the pillow off her cot, walked over and slammed him on the side of the head with it.

"What the hell was that for?" asked Tooley, coming up into a sitting position and rubbing his ear.

"You've got a lot of nerve coming on to me when you're married."

"I'm not coming on to you at the moment."

"But you did. You kissed me, you bastard!"

"I'd hardly call that adultery."

She slammed the pillow into him again, this time right across the eyes.

"Will you knock it off? I'm not married!"

"I could care less," said Bolivia, and was turning away when he grabbed the shirt and yanked her back.

"You always fly off the handle when you don't care about something?" he asked her.

"Frequently," said Bolivia.

He pulled her backward onto his lap, then grabbed her head and pulled it around. The next thing she knew he was kissing her, which was what she had wanted all along but hadn't known how to go about getting. She hadn't believed for a moment he was really married. She wasn't so stupid as to be attracted to a married man.

As she opened her mouth to him she reached around and loosened the scarf holding his hair, then pulled it so that his hair fell like a tent around their faces. In the light it seemed to give off a warm glow.

He started to twist her body, and when she realized what he had in mind, she did it without his help, lying back on the cot and pulling him down on top of her. She had no idea whether the cot would support two, but she figured she was about to find out.

With a sucking motion his lips parted from hers and she opened her eyes to his green gaze. "Do you think you could take off the helmet?" he asked her. "It's cutting into my scalp."

Bolivia grabbed her helmet and tossed it on the floor.

"And maybe the gun belt," said Tooley.

He lifted his torso so that she could unfasten the belt and drop it over the side of the cot.

"Anything else?" she asked.

"Anything you feel like getting rid of."

"I feel like getting rid of your shirt," said Bolivia, maneuvering her hands between them and attacking the buttons.

"Just my shirt?" asked Tooley.

"For starters."

When the shirt was opened she tilted her head for a moment to rub her nose in the thick, red pelt. It was like having a fur coat without having to kill the animal. She couldn't remember ever having taken a fancy to such a hairy man before, but she loved it. She unbuttoned her own shirt and spread it apart, then pulled his hairy chest down to rub against her breasts.

"That was one hell of a sexy move," said Tooley with a grin.

"You ain't seen nothing yet," she told him.

"I can hardly wait."

She lifted her face for another kiss, then wriggled around beneath him, wishing they were either on a large bed or the floor. The cot didn't leave much room for creativity.

She broke off the kiss for a moment, asking, "Are you wearing a gun belt?"

"No," said Tooley, his lips going to her neck.

"Then what's that—" She broke off, suddenly knowing exactly what it was that was poking into her. She felt the laughter moving through Tooley's body and felt a little stupid but not enough to keep her from wriggling around some more, the enjoyment of it now enhanced.

"Is this play-around time, or is this serious stuff?" Tooley asked her, his tongue moving lazily across her chest.

"It's play-around time," she said.

"That's what I figured."

"I wouldn't want you to think I was easy," she said, and he made a choking noise.

"You? *Easy?* Quit cracking me up, Bolivia."

"Maybe you'd like to gag me."

He lifted his head. "Maybe I would."

"You don't care to be entertained while you're making love?"

"Believe me, when we make love, that'll be entertainment enough."

She did believe him, and she felt a tremor go through her body at the thought of it. Maybe tonight. Late. When no one was likely to walk in on them. For now it was enough to let their bodies become acquainted. She could tell already that maybe their mouths were still at war, but their bodies had come to a sweet accommodation.

Anne was standing by the door to the glass elevator, looking impatient, when Sandy exited behind two fat tourists in polyester shorts. The air-conditioning in the store felt marvelous. She'd been on a stakeout in the back room of a liquor store for most of the day, and the temperature of the back room, sans air-conditioning, had been somewhere over one hundred ten degrees.

Anne looked gorgeous, as usual. Sandy always felt invisible when she was anywhere in public with Anne, except maybe on a baseball diamond. Even Annie didn't look gorgeous when they played ball, and it was the only time Sandy ever saw her sweat.

"You're late," said Anne, after first confirming the fact with her Rolex.

"I know. I'm sorry. I was involved in a shoot-out. And then I had to go home and shower and change..."

"That's no excuse," said Anne, then grinned. "I'm sorry, of course it's an excuse. My God, a shoot-out? You okay?"

What could she say? That shoot-outs weren't as scary as being late to meet Anne? "I'm okay."

Anne shook her head. "Things are getting bad when I think a dress fitting is up there in importance with a shoot-out. I'm sorry I snapped at you."

"It was a minor shoot-out. No one actually got shot." She looked around. She hadn't dressed correctly. Except for a few tourists, everyone in Neiman Marcus was dressed as though they were going to a dinner party, including Anne. She should've remembered Bal Harbour wasn't your usual mall.

"How're you doing?" Sandy asked her.

"I think I'm going round the bend," said Anne. "My mother has started to plan showers, the secretaries at the office want to have one for me, there are invitations to send, caterers to hire, Jack suddenly wants it videotaped... there are so many things, and all I wanted was a pretty dress."

"So buy yourself a pretty dress and elope in it."

"I did something worse. I moved the wedding up to a week from tomorrow."

"Annie, you'll never get everything done by then."

"I don't care. If I'm going to go crazy, I'd rather it only lasted another week rather than an entire month. Anyway, I work better under pressure."

The elevator stopped again on its way up and discharged some more passengers. All well dressed. Not one as tall as Bolivia. "Did Bolivia say she was going to be late?" asked Sandy.

"I didn't talk to her."

Sandy looked at her watch. "She should've been here half an hour ago. Bolivia's never late."

"I think, for Bolivia, this is rather like going to the dentist."

"Maybe she forgot."

"She never forgets anything."

"I haven't talked to her, either," said Sandy. "I've called her a couple of times, but she's never home."

"I thought you were going to the movies with her last night?"

"She didn't call, so I went home and conked out early."

"Come on, I'll show you the dress," said Anne. "You're the one who'll probably need alterations, anyway. They make dresses with bodies like Bolivia's in mind."

At least she didn't rub it in that Sandy usually shopped in the preteen department. But what the hell, the clothes were generally cheaper, and the fit was better. Some of her best buys had been made in the boys' department.

The dress was a disaster on Sandy. The waist was around her hips, and the skirt was two feet too long. She looked like a little kid dressing up in her mother's clothes.

"Can you picture what it'll look like when it's altered?" Anne asked her.

"No, I can't."

"It'll be fine, I promise."

"I wouldn't be insulted if you didn't want me as a bridesmaid, Annie, honest. I'd still come to your wedding."

"Are you backing out on me, too?"

"No, I just thought you might think—"

"You're going to be a bridesmaid, and I don't want to hear any more discussion about it."

Sandy stood very still as a woman pinned her dress in just about every place possible, then got back into her own clothes while Anne described Bolivia to the salesperson, who promised she'd keep an eye out for her. After that they took the elevator down to the first floor, where Sandy tried on straw hats. They decided on plain ones with upturned brims, which Anne said would look fine with a band of flowers around them. Sandy liked the hat.

"I'm starving," said Sandy.

"We'll give her until the store closes," Anne said. "You want to look at some lingerie with me?"

Sandy shrugged. She wore underwear, not lingerie, but she felt as if she had to make up for Bolivia's absence by being extra accommodating.

Tooley sat next to Bolivia at dinner that night. There was some good-natured kidding from the men, along the lines of, "Hey, Tooley, you go for boys these days?" with Tooley being friendly but not giving anything away. Bolivia didn't think they really knew anything was going on. She didn't think it likely that they'd think she had anything going for a guy who'd had her tied and gagged. At least, she hoped not.

They were just finishing supper when five men walked into the camp. Two were Americans dressed in civilian clothes but wearing them in a way that made them resemble uniforms. The other three were dressed as officers in some army Bolivia wasn't familiar with, but she assumed that they were Tamorons.

"Keep your helmet on and keep away from them," Tooley said to her in a low voice, and then he got up and joined the new arrivals.

"Don't worry," Bobby Joe whispered to her from across the table. "You look just like a guy. If they speak to you, though, lower your voice."

"I already have a low voice," said Bolivia.

"Not low enough."

Bolivia lowered her head and pretended to eat as she watched them out of the corner of her eye. They conferred for about five minutes and then they left, Tooley going with them.

"Who were they?" Bolivia asked.

"Those are our leaders," said Mason.

"I thought Tooley was your leader."

Mason shook his head. "He's more like a drill sergeant. I mean, we have to listen to him, but he has to listen to them."

Bolivia helped with KP without even being asked. It wasn't that she minded doing it; she just didn't like taking orders. Especially from men. Particularly from Tooley.

When the store closed at ten, Bolivia still hadn't shown up. "I'm really mad at her," said Anne. "I can't believe she'd do this to me."

"Maybe she's boycotting the wedding," Sandy said.

"Cute. But not out of the realm of possibility."

"Something must have come up," said Sandy. "She's never not met us before when she's supposed to."

"Well, I say we eat," said Anne.

They went to one of the restaurants and sat outside so that Bolivia would see them if she drove into the parking lot. They were almost close enough to her hotel to see it from their table.

They ordered drinks and Anne said, "If she doesn't come with me tomorrow, they'll never get the dresses ready on time."

"Relax, you said yourself she's built like a model."

"The size four ought to fit her perfectly."

"Come on," said Sandy, "let's forget about the wedding and have a good time."

"She didn't have her column in the paper today, either. I really think she's becoming undependable."

"Her column wasn't in?"

Anne nodded.

"Bolivia wouldn't miss a column."

"Well, she did. Jimmy Ryan had a column about the unrest in Overtown, instead."

"We're expecting some trouble there. What with the cutbacks in the city budget and the heat wave—"

"She's never missed a column."

"It's not like her," Sandy agreed.

"I'm telling you, she hasn't been herself lately, and it started when I told her about the wedding."

"Bolivia doesn't care about your wedding. She just likes to grouse."

"Then where is she?"

"You're starting to get me worried, Annie."

"You'd better worry, because I'm going to kill her when I see her."

"She wouldn't have just stood us up like this."

"Well, I don't see her here having a drink with us, do you?"

"Maybe she's in trouble."

Anne nodded. "She's in trouble all right."

"Maybe she went back to that jungle camp."

Anne's eyes widened. "You think she ran off with the redhead?"

"No. Running off with a man would be highly unlike Bolivia."

Anne nodded. "I'd do it before she would."

"So would I," said Sandy.

"I think this is her subtle way of telling me she doesn't want to be a bridesmaid."

"She doesn't have to be subtle about it—she told you straight out. I have a feeling something's wrong, and my feelings usually turn out to be correct." Sandy stood. "Come on, Annie, let's go. I want to check out her room."

"You're really getting nervous?"

"I really am."

Anne stood up. "Okay, I've lost my appetite anyway."

"Five card stud," called Bolivia, dealing the cards. She had a ten hidden and another one showing, and she tried to look nonchalant. After being burned a few times, though, the men didn't seem to be buying it any longer, because two of them immediately folded. Two more with face cards showing stayed with her, and Bobby Joe, the big loser, stayed in with a deuce. She'd like to give Bobby Joe a few basic lessons in poker, but not while he was in a game with her and she was winning all his money.

Bolivia's eyes kept returning to the path where Tooley had disappeared. It had been dark for a couple of hours already, and he still hadn't returned.

As she dealt again Mason said, "He's in a strategy session. It could go on all night."

*Betrayed*

"What're you talking about?" asked Bolivia, trying to act totally uninterested.

"You keep looking over at the path."

"Do I? I wasn't aware of it."

Some of the guys smiled outright at that. "Come on, admit it," said Bobby Joe. "You've got the hots for Tooley."

"You're very much mistaken," said Bolivia, throwing in her bet.

"Don't worry, I have a feeling it's mutual," he said.

"I don't know how you could possibly think I have the hots for a man who tied me up and gagged me."

"Some women get into that," said Mason.

"I'm not one of them," Bolivia insisted.

"Oh, we know you're tough," said Bobby Joe. "But the thing is, Tooley's really a good guy, and we figure you know that."

Bolivia ignored him as she dealt.

"We think you two are good together," said Mason. "It's about time Tooley had a woman."

"Well, it's not going to be me," said Bolivia, while at the same time she was wishing he'd get back so they could resume what they had started that afternoon.

She bet and two more of them dropped out. She dealt the last cards and now had two jacks showing. No one stayed in, which made her angry because she had wanted to flash her three jacks at them. The best hand all night, and no one even knew it.

She gathered the money, seeing that most of it was now in front of her. Well, they'd thought they were going to take her money, so she didn't feel sorry for them. Poker was her game, and she seldom lost.

Some of the guys stood and started to stretch. "Guess it's time to turn in," said Bobby Joe.

"But it's early," said Bolivia.

"Hell, Tooley had us on a twenty-mile hike today," said one of the guys.

"I'm beat," said Mason.

Bolivia felt like protesting that she had nothing to do all alone in the tent, but that would be as much as admitting that she was waiting for Tooley to get back. She gathered up her winnings, shoved then into her pockets and said goodnight to the guys.

Damn it, where was he? For hours she had been looking forward to being alone with him tonight, and instead he'd taken off. Well, the hell with him. Who needed him anyway?

Sandy used the spare key Bolivia had given her and opened the door to the hotel room.

"Leave the door open. It must be a hundred degrees in here," said Anne, turning on the overhead light.

Sandy went to the kitchen, a tiny area built into a closet, and checked for any food that might have been left out. Since Bolivia never ate at home, though, she wasn't surprised when she didn't find any. A look in the refrigerator turned up three cans of beer.

Anne went straight to the answering machine. She pushed the playback button and the next thing they heard was Sandy saying, "Give me a call when you get home."

The next twelve messages—which ran the tape out—were all from her boss, Henry. At first they were casual, things like. "When are you planning on dropping by work and saying hello?" but they soon became more angry, such as the one where he said, "Get your butt in here, Bolivia, or you're going to find yourself out of a job," and the last two sounded concerned. "At least give me a call," Henry said on the last one, "and let me know whether I should substitute something for your column. Bolivia? Are you okay?''

"I feel terrible," said Anne. "She could have been missing all week and we didn't even know it. Her best friends, and we didn't even know."

"Well, she wasn't taken from here by force," said Sandy. "I have a feeling she went on her own, which means she could have let us know and saved us from worry."

"Maybe she was in an accident."

Sandy shook her head. "We would've heard about an accident."

"What're we going to do?"

"We're going to that jungle camp," said Sandy.

"In the dark?"

"No, but first thing in the morning. And I'm talking early."

"Maybe we should call the police."

"What do you think *I* am?" Sandy reminded her.

"We don't even know where it is."

"It's wherever those women live who first complained to the paper. Henry ought to be able to tell us."

Anne started to blink. "I feel terrible. Here I was worried about my wedding, and Bolivia's in trouble."

"Don't cry yet," said Sandy. "You could be right, and she could've taken off with the redhead."

"But you don't think so, do you?"

Sandy shook her head. "No, I don't. And if she did run off without letting us know, I'm going to kill her."

*It was pitch dark in the tent. She heard the sound of the zipper opening on the flap, then heard him come inside. She knew it was Tooley by his smell: that animal odor of a man in heat.*

*In the silence of the night she heard other sounds: buttons being unfastened, the sound of a zipper, then the soft sounds of clothes being dropped to the ground. The temperature in the tent seemed to rise as she sensed him naked and lusty and only inches away from her.*

*She gave an involuntary moan and then heard him say, "Bolivia," his voice a low growl.*

*"Here," she said, throwing the blankets off her naked body and spreading her arms in anticipation.*

*The cot was too confining for him, though. He picked her up and then settled to the ground so that she was on top of him. The heat of her body merged with his, and his fur seemed to send off sparks.*

*"My love," he murmured, his hard mouth closing over hers, his tongue invading and fighting a small skirmish before taking command.*

*His hands were lighting fires on her body, and his aroused flesh was fighting to gain admittance when she lifted herself up, then came down with a vengeance. The shock of his size sent shudders through her; then her body seemed to expand to accept him, and they began the march to what was a foregone conclusion.*

"Bolivia? Are you awake?"

She came out of her reverie with a start. "What is it, Mason?"

"Has Tooley been back yet?"

"No."

"Okay. Sorry if I bothered you."

"That's okay, I couldn't get to sleep."

She sat up on her cot and glared at the empty one across the tent. Damn him for not coming back after she'd been looking forward to it all evening. Now she was too riled up by her daydream to even attempt to get to sleep.

She got up and took two more of the antibiotic pills Mason had given her, then decided to add a sleeping pill. It would serve Tooley right if he got back and found she was sound asleep.

The last laugh would be on him when he tried to wake her up.

## Chapter 11

"Hey, wake up." Tooley's voice came to her as though from a dream. She tried to reach out for him, but her arms were too heavy to move. *Come to bed with me,* she tried to say, but the words remained thoughts.

"Let's go, we're pulling out," he said, shaking her shoulder.

"It's the middle of the night," Bolivia protested, rolling away from his hand. She had been waiting for him all night, and now he wanted to *leave*? Anyway, she was too tired to even move. In a second she would have sunk back into sleep again.

"It's almost dawn."

Bolivia struggled to lift her lids. "Go away and let me sleep."

"Fine, but you'll miss the invasion."

She managed to get one eyelid halfway open. *"Now?"*

"Right now. You've got three minutes to get dressed and be outside. Come on, hustle. We're moving out."

*Betrayed* 173

"Why didn't you tell me?" she yelled at his retreating back, the unfairness of it striking her. "I wouldn't have taken a sleeping pill."

Bolivia lost Tooley at some point during the swift exodus from the camp. She stumbled down the dark path, her arms out in front of her to touch the other men and to help prevent a fall; more men were behind her, their hands reaching out in the same way. The ground was wet, and she could smell rain in the air. There must have been a storm while she had slept. She kept tripping on the exposed roots of trees as she tried to concentrate on waking up fully so that she could savor the adventure. She was unused to barbiturates and couldn't seem to shake off her grogginess.

When at last they emerged, it wasn't to the suburban street where she had parked her motorcycle—and that seemed so very long ago—but to an open field that appeared to be filled with trucks.

She looked quickly around for Tooley and didn't spot him. Someone shoved her back, and she followed the men in front of her into the nearest truck. They were packed in so tightly, they were practically in each other's laps, and once the truck started moving, Bolivia found that the warm bodies pressed against her and the motion of the truck combined to make her all the more sleepy. She fought it as long as she could, but at some point she must have succumbed, because the next thing she knew the truck was coming to a stop, and she felt people moving to get off.

They seemed to move as one unit so that she couldn't break through and look for Tooley. She could smell the ocean and see the false dawn in the sky. She followed the others down the ramp to a launch that quickly pulled off.

The fresh air revived her, and she looked around from where she sat among the others. She didn't see Tooley, but she saw Mason looking in her direction. He winked at her, and she relaxed. If she didn't see Tooley, she might be able to get away with going in with the invading troops. In fact, if she kept her head down, he wouldn't be likely to spot her.

The thought of putting one over on Tooley made her smile. With the thought that she was well on her way into the biggest adventure of her life, her adrenaline began to flow.

"I'm starved," she muttered.

One of the men next to her handed her a candy bar, and she wordlessly began to devour it.

Anne saw the look of metal glinting in the undergrowth and brought her Jaguar to a stop at the side of the road. "Just a second," she said to Sandy, as she got out of the car and walked over to the mangroves. There, shoved behind some bushes, was Bolivia's motorcycle.

Anne looked around to call to Sandy, but she was already beside her. "You were right," Anne said.

Sandy seemed as unnerved by the sight of the cycle as Anne. "I wish I hadn't been."

"Maybe she's just camping out, having a good time."

"She wouldn't have just left her cycle like that," Sandy said.

"We should've realized sooner."

Sandy was trying to see through the thick mangroves. "She's got to be in there somewhere."

"Do you have your gun with you?" Anne asked her.

"Of course."

"Although I don't see what good it's going to be against a bunch of crazy guys with rifles and machine guns. Maybe rocket launchers, for all we know."

"Probably no good," Sandy admitted. "But I told my partner where we were going, and if he doesn't hear from me within an hour, he's coming in with help."

"Maybe we ought to wait for him."

"Since when did you become so chicken, Annie?"

Anne turned a dismayed face toward her. "I have gotten chicken, haven't I? I guess since I fell in love."

Sandy patted her hand. "Hey, it's okay. You didn't chicken out when Jack needed you, and you won't now. If I know you, it's the bugs you're afraid of, anyway."

Anne opened her handbag and took out a spray can of Raid. "Bugs I'm prepared for."

Sandy opened the door. "Lock up, and let's go."

It looked dark and damp and creepy and crawling with bugs, and probably other things. Anne followed Sandy in, glad she'd put socks on and long pants and a shirt with long sleeves. It was an unfamiliar part of Florida to her, and she could understand why people wanted to tear it down, drain the water and develop it.

Sandy came to a stop, and Anne watched her reach down and pick something up. Whatever it was, it had a glint to it. "What's that?" she asked her.

Sandy held it out for her to see. "It's a shell. Looks like it's from an M-16."

"I don't want to hear that."

Sandy shrugged. "Bolivia said they had rifles. Anyway, it's no big deal. Everyone and his neighbor owns a gun in Florida."

"Bolivia doesn't."

"It's not likely she's been shot, Annie. If she'd sensed that kind of danger, she wouldn't have gone back a second time."

Anne disagreed. "Bolivia thrives on danger."

"But she's not stupid."

"Any woman can become stupid when it comes to a man."

"Just keep that thought. Maybe she and the redhead are even now wheeling off into the sunset together."

"It's dark and damp and creepy in here."

"I'll bet Bolivia loves it," said Sandy.

"Yeah."

"She'll pretend she's in Central America and get off on it."

"We've been walking for an awfully long time."

"Let's pick up the pace," said Sandy, sounding more uneasy than she was willing to admit.

When they reached a large clearing they found the smoldering remains of a camp fire. Sandy reached out an arm and halted Anne's progress. "Stay here while I look around," she said.

"I'll help you."

"I don't want you destroying any evidence."

Anne turned a little pale. "Evidence of what?"

"You're a lawyer, you figure it out."

"I want to help."

"Just give me a couple of minutes and then you can help, okay?"

Anne ignored the advice and followed her, being careful to walk in Sandy's footprints. Whoever had cleared out had done a pretty good job of covering up that they'd been there, but Sandy pointed out evenly spaced holes where tent posts had been, and there were dozens of shells scattered around.

The most disquieting piece of evidence was found by Anne. She found a pair of white cotton panties covered in mud beneath some leaves she had kicked aside.

She held them up, and Sandy came over to take a look. "They could belong to anyone," said Sandy.

"Bolivia always wears cotton pants. She's the only woman I know who doesn't wear bikinis."

"Kids probably play in here."

"The mothers around here aren't going to let their daughters play in here, and they're girls' pants."

"I just don't think we should jump to any conclusions."

"Like rape and murder?"

"Annie, Bolivia's pretty tough."

"I know."

"Let's go," said Sandy. "Whoever was here is gone now. I think it's time to get some help on this."

A few minutes later the launches pulled up to a large ship anchored some distance from shore. Along with some of the others, Bolivia stood to get a look at it.

It didn't look like a naval ship, but it also didn't look like a cruise ship. If anything, it looked like the kind of ship that transported things. It had a huge deck and not much depth, and if it had a name, it sure wasn't painted on the side. The sun was coming up, and Bolivia pulled her helmet down to obscure as much of her face as possible.

It wasn't only because of the men in charge—whoever they were—it was also to keep Tooley from seeing her at this point. She hunched down so that she was the same height as the men around her, then followed them to the gangplanks, which were now being put in place. She figured she ought to be able to get lost in a ship as big as that. Tooley would have a heart attack, but what the hell, she was a reporter, and this was a story. And it would be a much better story if she weren't left behind on the ship, which had probably been Tooley's intention.

She stepped onto the deck and stayed close to the others who were making their way to the back and then settling down on the deck. She sat cross-legged like the others, her head down. And then, from somewhere, coffee was passed around. Did they send out for coffee before invasions? She took the cup that was offered her and took a couple of sips, then realized it might be hours before she had the use of a bathroom, unless she wanted to fake it standing up. Reluctantly, she handed the cup to the guy next to her, who was happy to relieve her of it.

As the sun rose higher in the sky, the air became hotter and more humid. She had always found it cooler being out on the water on a boat, but this one seemed to be moving at a snail's pace, much too slowly to stir up any air. When clouds started to cover the sun she was happy at first for the diminished temperature, but then a sudden storm whipped up out of nowhere, and as rain quickly drenched them, the boat began rocking from the motion of the waves.

All around her men were starting to get up and fight their way to the rails. The sounds and stench of their vomiting carried, and at first Bolivia thought it would make her sick. But as more and more men got sick, she felt less and less inclined in that direction. She wasn't prone to motion sickness of any kind, and her luck seemed to be holding.

Just about everyone was standing by now, so Bolivia got to her feet. She was as tall as or taller than most of the men, so she hunched down, pulling her shoulders in around her face. Then she heard his voice; it was unmistakable.

She kept her head lowered but lifted her eyes. He was half a foot taller then anyone else on the ship, and his head could be clearly seen across the deck. With his red hair and in other clothes, on another kind of ship, he would look like an ancient Viking warrior come to life. Just the sight of him was enough to raise her body temperature, and she wondered why, out of all the men in the world, this one should hold such a strong physical attraction for her. If this was anything like love, she was beginning to understand Annie's wanting to spend the rest of her life with Jack.

Annie! My God, she was supposed to meet Annie and Sandy tonight. Or was it last night? It was going to take a lot of explaining to square this one with Annie. She could only hope her exclusive would explain it for her. Annie was going to be furious, though, and blame it all on Bolivia's reluctance to be in the wedding.

She felt someone's eyes on her and lifted her head for a moment. She found herself staring straight at Tooley, still the width of the boat away from her but now starting to move in her direction.

She quickly scrunched down and began to move in closer to some of the men. There were empty spaces, and most of the men huddled close to the rail. She quickly put her hand on her stomach to mimic seasickness and started to shove her way through the crowd to get to the rail. Some of them shoved back, but some of them recognized her and allowed her through.

When she got to the rail she hung her head over, trying to blend in with everyone else. She was sure she had succeeded until a hand grabbed the back of her shirt and gave a tug. She hung on to the rail with both hands, hoping the shirt wouldn't get torn from her back. She felt the fabric being released and breathed a sigh of relief, but in the next second someone had hold of her upper arms and was pulling her back with more force than she could hold out against.

She let go of the rail and felt them both stumble backward; then she turned to see Tooley's familiar grin.

"I thought I'd lost you," he said.

Bolivia eyed him warily, wishing he would go away and let her get lost again.

"Seasick, huh? I guess I'm the only one on board who isn't."

"I wasn't sick," said Bolivia.

"Then what were you doing hanging over the rail?"

"Trying to get away from you!"

A glint of understanding came into his eyes. "Oh, no—no way!"

"I don't see why I can't—"

"You're lucky to even be here. I'd be in deep trouble if the big guns knew about it."

"Maybe I'll just scream and give away the game."

"Maybe I'll just slip another gag into that sexy mouth of yours."

"You usually refer to it as big."

"Oh, it's that all right, but it's also sexy, and right now it's driving me nuts."

His eyes were on her mouth now, and her own mouth suddenly softened. She felt the rise in temperature again, felt the way her face was involuntarily tipping up toward his.

He looked momentarily tempted, but then he forcibly turned her away from him and propelled her forward.

"What're you doing?" she muttered.

"Just keep going in that direction," he said, one of his fingers locked in her gun belt as his other hand directed her.

"Where are we going?"

"No questions. Just keep your mouth shut and your head down."

She wanted to stop and give him an argument, but something about the way his hand felt on her back kept her moving. They were almost to the front of the boat when he let go of her and stepped past her, then pointed the way down a spiral metal ladder.

"What's down there?" Bolivia asked.

"No questions," said Tooley. "Just go down and act like you know where you're going."

"It would be easier if I did know," she muttered, but not before taking the first few steps downward.

She emerged in what she took to be the engine room. She didn't see anyone around, and Tooley quickly joined her and took her arm, moving her quickly down a passageway. When they came to a door he opened it and shoved her inside.

Before he closed the door, leaving them in total darkness, she had time to see that it was a small enclosure, no more than two feet by two feet and maybe eight feet tall, and hanging from one wall were a mop and a broom.

"What the hell do you think you're doing?" she yelled, sure that he was going to tie her up here and leave her until the invasion was over.

Tooley put his arms around her and pulled her close. "What I've wanted to do since the first moment you walked into our camp."

"Here? *Now?*"

"We could die in the invasion, we could miss our chance forever," he said, his hands moving up under her shirt and causing shock waves to roll through her system.

"I have no intention of dying—"

"Will you just shut up and let me make love to you, for God's sake?"

And then his lips were silencing hers, and he was pressing her up against the wall. Her arms went around his waist and then moved down, pulling him even closer to her as she gave in to what she had wanted to do since she had first seen him. What she had daydreamed about, fantasized, what she had tried to deny at times, but never successfully.

The kiss was long and hard and devouring. The adrenaline was flowing even as her limbs were melting, her tongue was moving hungrily against his, and his hands were making rapid explorations of her body.

When she felt his hands loosening her gun belt and heard it fall to the floor, followed quickly by expert fingers unbuttoning her pants and shoving them downward, she pulled her mouth away for a moment, gasping for air. "In a *broom* closet?" she felt compelled to complain, even though she was secretly thrilled.

His own pants were already dropping when he said, "You have a better idea?"

*A broom closet?* she was still wondering as he entered her and the detonation from the joining jolted her.

My God, the first time they made love, and they were doing it in a broom closet! It would be something to tell their grandchildren about, that on the day of the invasion... well, it really wasn't the kind of thing she could tell children... not the kind of thing she could tell anyone, really... but just exactly the kind of thing she could thoroughly enjoy at the moment and always remember as the most novel, the most romantic, the most spectacular... the most... oh, God, she couldn't even describe it anymore....

He held on to her tightly, his breath coming in gasps. She collapsed against the wall, holding him for dear life as the enormity of the experience flowed through her. So this was how it could actually be, and to think she hadn't had a clue. It was almost enough to make her forget about the invasion.

"If we don't get out of this alive," Tooley started to say, but she put her hand over his mouth.

"Don't even think it," she told him.

He bit her finger until she removed her hand. "Anything could happen. You never know."

"Not to me," said Bolivia. "At the moment I'm feeling rather immortal."

She heard his chuckle. "I'm feeling just as immortal, my love, but in the event we don't make it—"

"Just shut up about that!"

"Damn it, Bolivia, I'm trying to declare my love, and you're telling me to shut up!"

"Your love?"

"Yes."

"Oh. Well, go ahead."

"Forget it!"

"Why don't you just gag me?"

"I'm thinking about it."

While he was thinking about it she kissed him again. They could declare their love later; right now she'd rather make love again while they still had the opportunity.

Anne pulled into the parking lot of the police station in downtown Miami.

"Park anywhere," said Sandy, already opening the door.

"I want to go with you."

"No, you wait here. Or go across the street and get some coffee, if you want. Believe me, it's preferable to where you'd have to wait inside."

"Okay, I'll be getting coffee," said Anne. "But don't be too long. I'm worried."

"If I'm longer than a half hour," said Sandy, "send the National Guard in after me."

Barney at the desk told her the lieutenant was in, so Sandy headed upstairs. She was going to lay out the facts for Lieutenant Perez and ask for his help. And if he wouldn't give it? Then she'd just have to do something on her own.

The lieutenant was standing by the coffee machine when she entered the squad room. He saw her and said, "What're you doing in here on your day off, McGee?"

"I need to talk to you, Lieutenant."

"Sure. Come on in my office."

She followed him inside and waited while he sat behind his desk. She was too nervous to take one of the chairs. "A friend of mine has disappeared," she said. "And something strange seems to be going on."

"Tell me about it."

She did, including everything she could remember, and ending up with a description of the jungle camp.

"Back up a little," said the lieutenant, "and tell me about the missing person's report."

She repeated what she had been told, that the government had said to stay out of it.

Lieutenant Perez got on the phone, and she could hear him asking someone for the missing person's report. While they were waiting for it he said, "Reporters, though, they take off all the time on stories, don't they?"

"She's not that kind of reporter, Lieutenant. She writes a weekly column for the *Times*."

"What's her name?"

"Bolivia Smith."

His face got tense at the name. "That the one who's always looking for police corruption?"

"Only if it's there," said Sandy.

"Yeah. You're right. But some of those reporters don't care whether it's there or not, they just want a story."

"Not Bolivia." Sandy tried to assure him.

Someone from Missing Persons brought in the report and handed it to the lieutenant.

"What's this?" asked the lieutenant.

"Just what it looks like," said the policewoman.

"We were told to stay out of this?"

"That's right."

The policewoman left, and Lieutenant Perez said, "I'll make a couple of phone calls, find out what the story is."

Sandy started to sit down.

"In private," said the lieutenant.

"I'll be right outside," said Sandy.

Five minutes later the lieutenant opened the door to his office and asked her to come inside.

"What did you find out?" she asked him.

"I'm sorry, McGee, but I'm afraid I'm going to have to ask you for your gun and your shield."

"What?" Was this a joke or something?

"I'm sorry."

"What's going on here?" she asked, backing away from his desk.

"I'd rather not have to take them from you forcibly."

"What's the charge here?"

"If it's any reassurance, I'm sure your friend is all right."

"Reassurance? Your arresting me is going to make me feel reassured about Bolivia?"

"We're not arresting you. You're just being detained for twenty-four hours."

Sandy was halfway out the door when she heard the lieutenant on the phone calling for assistance. What was she going to do, try to escape from the cops she worked with? Maybe get shot trying?

Totally frustrated she turned back into the lieutenant's office and handed over her shield and her handgun. It was going to be up to Annie now.

Bolivia hadn't realized how noisy it was until the engines were cut. Suddenly there was dead silence in the broom closet, with only the sound of some rather heavy breathing.

"Why'd they cut the engines?" she asked. She had rather lost count of the time, but not so much that they could have reached Tamoros yet.

"We're switching to fishing boats."

She could feel Tooley pulling up his pants and followed suit. "Fishing boats?"

"They're going to know they're being invaded if they spot a ship this size approaching the island."

"We're going to need a lot of fishing boats," said Bolivia, thinking of the hundreds of men on deck.

"We've got a lot."

"The guys are going to get even sicker on those," said Bolivia. "Some invasion, a lot of seasick soldiers."

Tooley opened the door a crack and looked outside. "Stay close to me now, and keep your head down. If anyone asks anything, I'll answer the questions."

"Right," said Bolivia, fastening her gun belt.

"We're going to be going in on the last boat."

"Why the last? How are you going to lead an invasion if you're on the last boat?"

"Who said *I* was leading it," said Tooley.

"You're not?"

"Hell no!"

"I thought you were the commander or whatever."

"I was training them, that's all. I'm not going to risk my butt in the front lines."

"Isn't that what you're getting paid for?"

"Not in my book," said Tooley, leaving the closet and heading down the passageway.

A bewildered Bolivia followed. She still didn't know whether he was in it for the money or because he was government, but either way he wasn't sounding as gung ho as he had seemed before. For a moment she had the idea that maybe making love to her had changed him, that now he had something to live for.

She dismissed that idea pretty quickly. Whatever his motive for staying out of the action was, she was sure it had nothing to do with her.

Anne took her time over two cups of coffee, then finally ordered breakfast. She figured if Sandy was taking so long she must be accomplishing something. It made her feel helpless, though, having to wait while Sandy did everything. As an attorney she was used to taking charge herself.

She dawdled over breakfast, but after an hour and a half had passed and still no Sandy, she began to worry. Although what she had to worry about when Sandy was safe in a police station, she didn't know. And yet something started to nag her, telling her to do something.

She finally got some change from the cashier and went to the pay phone at the back of the diner and called the police station.

She asked for Sandy and was told it was her day off.

"I know it's her day off, but she's in there," said Anne. "Would you mind checking?"

She was put on hold for a good five minutes, and then Lieutenant Perez came on the line. Anne knew the name, because Sandy often talked about him. "I'm looking for Sandy," she told him.

"She's not in today," said the lieutenant.

"She went in there over an hour and a half ago and hasn't come out yet," said Anne.

"I think you're mistaken, miss."

"I'm not mistaken. I was with her. I'm still waiting for her."

"I don't know, maybe she came in for something and left. Probably forgot about you."

"That's just not possible, Lieutenant. We're looking for a friend of ours."

The lieutenant was silent for a moment. "Where are you calling from?"

"What difference does that make?"

"Is this an outside call?"

"I'm just trying to find out where Sandy is."

"If you'll stay where you are, I'll have someone come and talk to you."

Anne suddenly didn't like what she was hearing at all. Something was wrong, and she could swear the lieutenant was part of it.

She hung up the phone and quickly paid her bill. As she was heading across the street to the parking lot, she saw several uniformed officers coming out of the building. She stopped midway in the cross walk and turned around. She didn't start running until she got around the corner.

Tooley went up the ladder first, with Bolivia behind him. Once on the deck she ducked into a group of men and scrunched down so he couldn't see her. She saw him look around for her, then head back to the ladder. As soon as he did she started snaking her way through the men who were pressing forward to disembark.

Maybe Tooley didn't want to be in one of the first boats, but she did. She wanted to be a part of the excitement, the danger, the action. She wanted to be able to file the best damn story the *Times* had ever printed.

And after that she wanted to be with Tooley again.

Anne made it all the way to the *Times* building on foot. A part of her knew how disreputable she looked, and she hated looking bad in public, but the larger part of her was too worried to care.

She took the elevator up to the editorial offices to look for Henry. She wasn't sure whether he worked on Saturdays and was relieved to find him in.

"My name's Anne Larkin," she told him. "I'm a friend of Bolivia's."

"Where the hell is she?" asked Henry.

"I don't know. That's what I want to see you about."

It took her a long time to tell the whole story, particularly since Henry kept interrupting and asking her to clarify points.

When she was finished he said, "Wait outside my office. I'm going to make a few calls to Washington."

Anne nodded and went outside. She thought of finding Bolivia's office and looking for clues, but she had a feeling that the only clues of any importance were the ones they had found at the jungle camp. She was still debating when Henry called her back into his office and asked her to close the door.

"What's the matter?" she asked him, unnerved by the serious expression on his face.

"I suppose it's too much to ask you to go home and forget about it?" he said.

"What is 'it'?"

Henry studied her for a moment, then seemed satisfied with what he saw. "You're that lawyer friend of hers, aren't you?"

Anne nodded.

"I was told in no uncertain terms, but by someone pretty high up, that I'd better back off for reasons of national security."

"That's ridiculous," said Anne.

"That's what I said."

"What could Bolivia possibly have to do with national security?"

"What you should be asking is what that jungle camp has to do with it."

"Isn't there anything we can do?"

Henry shrugged. "I can't think of anything except sit by the phone and hope Bolivia calls in."

"That's not good enough," said Anne. "Could I borrow your car?"

"Where are you planning on going?"

"Back to that jungle camp. No one's there now, but someone must have seen them leave."

"Never mind borrowing it," said Henry. "I'm going with you."

## Chapter 12

"I'm Ned Copper, and this is Newsline. Tonight, the invasion of Tamoros. With us live in the studio is Bolivia Smith, the reporter with the Miami Times *who actually went along on the invasion.*"

The camera panned to Bolivia. This was where the guests usually smiled, but Bolivia thought it befitted a war correspondent to look serious, so she merely nodded.

Ned smiled at her. He was better looking in person, although maybe she had acquired a predilection for redheads. He was also shorter.

"Tell us, Bolivia, just how you got involved in the invasion of Tamoros?"

"Well, Ned, it started out as just another story for my weekly column."

"And ended up putting you strongly in contention for the Pulitzer prize."

She gave a modest smile while at the same time wondering if he was going to make a habit of interrupting her. "There were complaints about a group of veterans camping out in a jungle area in Fort Lauderdale—"

He chimed in with, "At what point did you learn our government was involved?"

"Not until the actual invasion was under way, although I had my suspicions from the start. A woman had gone to the police and filed a missing person's report—"

"We're going to have to take a break here, Bolivia, and when we get back I'm going to ask you about the part you personally played in the invasion."

He swung around in his chair, turning his back to her while a commercial was being aired. She wanted to ask him why he kept interrupting her but couldn't quite get up her nerve.

When the show resumed, Ned said, "We've also got with us tonight, in our New York newsroom, Jim O'Toole, the man who led the invasion. Good evening, Jim."

"Hi, Ned."

Bolivia heard the voice but couldn't see him. "He didn't lead the invasion," she spoke up.

"I'm sorry, what was that?" asked Ned.

"Hi, Bolivia," came Tooley's voice, loud and clear.

"I said he didn't lead the invasion," said Bolivia. "Actually, he brought up the rear. The extreme rear. I should know. I was at the front of the lines."

"Ask her about the broom closet, Ned," said Tooley.

Bolivia froze in her seat. It wasn't possible. He wouldn't have the nerve to bring up the broom closet live, on national TV, with millions of viewers, including relatives of hers.

*Betrayed*

"What's this about a broom closet?" asked Ned, pouncing on it as if it had some news value.

Bolivia looked straight into the camera and said. "The invading forces moved into the capital city of Tamoros—"

"Bolivia and I made love in the broom closet," said Tooley, and she could tell by his voice that he was grinning.

"Wasn't that rather uncomfortable?" asked Ned.

"This is my fantasy," yelled Bolivia, "and I wish you'd stay out of it, Tooley."

"I thought we were in this together," he said.

"A broom closet," mused Ned, clearly uncomfortable with the idea.

"You trying to avoid me, Bolivia?" asked Tooley.

Bolivia felt something poking her in the back, and then, in a whisper, he said, "You can't get away from me that easily."

Bolivia swiveled her head around and saw Tooley crowded in behind her on the deck of the fishing boat. She glared at him before turning back around.

"Thought you'd lost me, huh?"

"Get away from me," said Bolivia.

"You're not going anywhere without me."

She moved around so that they were face-to-face. The other men didn't have to hear what she had to say to him. "I don't happen to be chicken like you are. I want to be one of the first ones in."

"You calling me chicken?"

"You're either a mercenary who isn't earning his pay or a chicken government agent."

"And what are you, a potential suicide?"

"I'm not afraid!"

"That's because your brains are in your feet!"

"Which is where your guts are," countered Bolivia, almost nose to nose with him, her words more a hiss than a whisper.

"You weren't talking like that in the closet," said Tooley, his green eyes practically throwing sparks.

"We're not in the closet now," said Bolivia, looking around to see if anyone could overhear them. They were garnering some looks, but most of the men were talking among themselves.

"You've got a choice, Bolivia," said Tooley. "Of course, I've given you choices before, and you always seem to pick the wrong ones."

"I've made my choice."

"Just listen to me. Now, you're either going to promise to stay by my side, or I'm going to order this boat to turn back, and you'll be reduced to hearing about the invasion on the radio after the fact."

"Turn it around. Big deal," said Bolivia, calling his bluff.

"Is that your final answer?"

"That's it."

He got up, still bluffing, and carefully picked his way between the men seated on the deck. She still thought he was bluffing, even when she saw him talking to the man at the wheel.

When the boat started to turn in the water, though, she wasn't so sure. Damn it, the man was as stubborn as she was.

Anger started to replace the adrenaline in her body, and by the time Tooley was again seated in front of her, she was beside herself with rage.

"Why did you do that?" she demanded.

"It was your choice, Bolivia."

"All right, I'll stay by your side."

"I wonder why I don't believe you." Tooley tilted his head back as though trying to get a suntan on his face.

"You've got your promise. That isn't fair."

"I have a feeling you're not above lying to me."

Bolivia crossed her heart and held her hand up.

"We're not children now," he said.

Maybe she could jump off the boat and swim to one of the others. She started to get up, but Tooley grabbed her and forced her back down.

He grinned at her. "I tell you what, how about swearing by your love for me?"

"I don't recall telling you I loved you."

"You didn't have to. It was obvious."

"How do you know I don't make love to everyone in a broom closet?"

Tooley shrugged. "Then swear by it, and if you don't love me, you can feel free to break your oath."

Bolivia avoided his eyes. "I don't want to."

"That proves you love me." The bastard was gloating now.

So she loved him? So what? What did that have to do with an invasion?

"Look at you, you're blushing."

Bolivia glared at him. "I don't blush."

"Then you'd better cover your face, 'cause you're getting sunburnt."

Bolivia tugged her helmet down so she didn't have to look at him.

"Come on," said Tooley. "Admit it."

"Maybe I do," said Bolivia, trying to sound extremely casual about it, "but it's hard to tell, given the circumstances we've been in."

"What do you mean? The circumstances have been perfect. Love is never as glorious as when it's under wartime conditions."

"Is that what you found in Vietnam?"

Tooley made a noise in his throat. "Look, I'll forget your past if you'll forget mine."

"That's not fair. I have a feeling your past is far more extensive."

Tooley chuckled. "I've heard about reporters, how they'll do anything for a story."

"You heard wrong."

"Really? It seems to me you let yourself get tied up and gagged for a story."

"There are limits to what I'll do for a story," Bolivia informed him.

"Really? Name one."

"You're getting off the subject, Tooley."

"I'd like to hear what your limits are."

"You're testing them at the moment."

"By asking you to swear by your love for me?"

"If you really loved me, Tooley, you'd take my word for it. I already promised I'd stay with you."

"It's not *my* love that's being called into question here. I already declared my love in the broom closet."

She might as well put an end to it now, otherwise she had a feeling she was going to hear about that broom closet for the rest of her life. "Yes," she countered, "but words uttered in the heat of passion don't count."

"On the contrary, I think people are at their most honest then."

"I disagree. I think that very often one mistakes passion for love."

Tooley shook his head. "Maybe addle-minded people do. I don't. Take now, for instance. I'm feeling very much like strangling that pretty little neck of yours, but at the same time, I know I love you."

"You sound confused to me, Tooley. You sound like you need psychiatric counseling."

"You're driving me there."

And she was loving every minute of it. Somehow, making Tooley angry was more fun than putting anyone else in a good mood. And he loved her. He must, or he wouldn't keep talking about it.

Bolivia looked him in the eye. "If, when this is all over, the danger past, everything back to normal, you say to me, *I love you, Bolivia*, then I'll believe you."

"I was letting you know earlier than I might have in case I got killed. I'd hate to go to my grave without your knowing. It's kind of special to me because I've never told a woman that I loved her before."

Bolivia snorted with laughter.

He gave her a sheepish look. "Not when I've meant it, anyway."

"That was a pretty little speech, Tooley, but it lacked a certain validity, since you know very well you're not going to your grave. You seem determined to stay away from the front lines."

"Obviously you know nothing about guerilla warfare. Whether in the front or the back, we could be ambushed at any time."

"I know enough about guerilla warfare to know *we're* the guerillas in this one, Tooley, and any ambushing will be done by us, not the Tamoron army, whom we're taking unawares."

"You know, if we end up together, Bolivia, I wonder whether this strong urge to gag you will ever abate."

"Every time I show some sign of having a superior intelligence to yours, you want to gag me."

"If that were the case, you never would have been gagged."

Bolivia drew her head back. "Did I hear you correctly?"

"I'm sure you did."

"Are you saying that I'm not as intelligent as you are?"

"It's not an insult, Bolivia, merely a fact."

She got to her feet and looked down at him. "I've changed my mind. I'll swear that oath now on my love for you." She no longer had any qualms about it, because she'd just fallen out of love with him. Of all the conceited, egotistical—

Tooley got to his feet, looking as if he wanted to hug her. "I'll be right back, sweetheart," he said. "I've got to tell the captain to turn around again."

Anne felt like saying, *Stop the car, Henry, and let me drive,* but she didn't think it would be politic. Not when it was his car and he was good enough to go off with her on what was probably a wild-goose chase to find Bolivia. But oh, was he slow. There was a fifty-five mph speed limit on 1-95, he was barely doing fifty; everyone else was passing them.

It was over an hour before they reached the block in Fort Lauderdale where Bolivia's motorcycle was parked. Anne saw children playing in their front yards and men washing cars as Henry pulled up to the curb.

"You go up the block, I'll go down," said Henry. "Find out if anyone saw anything."

"I know how to question witnesses," Anne told him.

"Yeah, sure you do. Sorry."

Everyone Anne questioned said the same thing. No one had seen anyone go into or out of the jungle in the last couple of days. They figured the publicity in the *Times* had gotten rid of them.

When Anne and Henry met back at the car to compare notes he said, "Well, I guess they didn't come out here. Let's take a drive, see just how big that area is."

They headed west, but the road dead-ended up against a canal after a couple of miles. Henry made a U-turn and headed back where they'd been. Going east, though, and then south, they came to the end of the mangrove jungle where it flattened out into a field. Henry parked and got out of the car to take a look.

When he came back he said, "There's been a lot of traffic through there. You can see tire tracks all over the place."

"Kids probably come here to drag race," said Anne.

"I don't think so. It looks pretty recent."

For a really ugly area there were a couple of very large homes just across the field. Anne understood why when they drove around that way and saw that the houses backed up to a lake. Rich people always wanted to live on the water.

"I guess we ought to question them," said Henry. "I'll take Tara, you take the Moorish castle."

Anne was very conscious of the way she looked when she walked up to the door and rang the bell. If she lived in a house like this, she wouldn't answer the door to someone who looked like her. On the other hand, they probably had servants to answer the door. After three rings, not even a servant had answered.

She walked around to the back of the house. It could be they were out on their patio, or maybe their boat. In a house like this they had to have a yacht.

She didn't see anyone on the patio, and the yacht, if there was one, was gone. She did see a gardener, though, in shorts and a straw hat.

"Is anyone home?" Anne called out to him.

The man looked up but didn't say anything.

She approached him in case he was hard of hearing. "Are the owners of the house around?"

He shrugged and shook his head. Close up he looked Cuban, or maybe Mexican, and she switched to Spanish.

This time she got an answer. The people who owned the house were out on their boat for the day and weren't expected back for hours.

"I wonder if you could help me," said Anne. "That area over there," she said, pointing, "the one that looks like a jungle..."

He nodded.

"Have you seen anyone coming out of there lately?"

His head bobbed up and down.

"When?"

Early that morning, he told her, when it was still dark. He said he sometimes started work very early so that he'd finish before the sun got too hot. There had been many of them, and they'd been carrying guns.

"How many?" asked Anne.

"I don't know, but many dozens."

"What were they doing?" asked Anne.

"They were getting into trucks, and then later I heard the trucks pull off."

"Do you know anything about them?"

He shook his head. "Just that some of them are Tamorons."

"How do you know that?"

He pointed to himself. "Because I am Tamoron and I heard some of them speak."

That was all he knew, and Anne thanked him before heading for the front of the house. She saw Henry already inside the car and went over and got in.

"I drew a blank," said Henry.

"I didn't. I talked to a gardener who saw a lot of men with guns getting into trucks this morning."

"Did he say how many?"

"Many dozens."

"That's a strange way of putting it."

"He didn't speak English. He's Tamoron, and he says some of the men were, too."

"Probably illegal aliens hiding out in there. Maybe it was the INS picking them up."

"I don't think so. He said the men were carrying guns."

"Maybe Tamorons are planning an attack on Fort Lauderdale."

"None of it makes sense," said Anne. "Bolivia didn't mention illegal aliens, and she didn't mention Tamorons. The man she kept talking about—Tooley—was American. She said they were Vietnam vets."

"And what would Vietnam vets have in common with Tamorons?" mused Henry. "I think...I think we may be on to a story here."

"We're trying to find Bolivia."

"Ah, but if there's a story to be had, Bolivia would want to be in the middle of it."

Anne shook her head. "If it was Contras, or if it was Cubans—"

"Tamoros is even more in the news these days," said Henry. "What if...what if they were on their way back to Tamoros to effect another coup?"

"You mean an invasion?"

"Exactly," said Henry.

"And our government's involved?"

"It would seem so."

"We don't have any proof, Henry. All we have is a gardener who saw some men with guns getting on trucks, and Bolivia, who's disappeared."

"Not yet we don't," said Henry, starting up the car.

"Where are we going?"

"To the harbor. Maybe we can find someone who saw them getting on boats."

"Can I make a phone call first? I was supposed to meet my fiancé two hours ago, and he's going to have a search party out looking for me pretty soon."

Henry moved his jacket from the center of the seat and revealed a car phone. "Be my guest," he said.

Most of the men were asleep on the deck. Bolivia wished she could get to sleep, but she was too uncomfortable, and the sun was blisteringly hot.

"Try to get some rest," Tooley told her.

"If I could use your lap, I might be able to."

"I think if you used my lap you'd get more attention than we want. You're supposed to be a guy, you know."

"Like it couldn't happen."

"Listen, I have a macho image to maintain."

"*Image?* Is that all you think it is?"

Tooley grinned. "Are you trying to tell me you find me extremely manly?"

"'Manly' wasn't the word," said Bolivia. "I think the word was 'macho,' and yes, I find you macho. Overly macho, if you want to know the truth."

"You're not exactly the sweet young maiden of folklore."

"You weren't complaining in the broom closet."

"I'm not complaining now," said Tooley. "But it takes someone like me to handle someone like you."

Bolivia instantly went on red alert. "Did you say *handle*?"

"Manage, control, whatever you want to call it." He said it blithely, but the glint in his eyes told her that he knew he was getting to her.

"You honestly think you can handle me, Tooley?"

"I think I've made quite a bit of progress."

"Yes, with rope and a gag!"

"Calm down, Bolivia—"

"Don't you dare tell me what to do, you obnoxious, egocentric, overbearing—"

"I love you, too, sweetie."

They almost struck out at the harbor. Then, just as they were leaving, a man walking toward them on the dock happened to ask, "You people know why the place was closed off this morning?"

Henry and Anne stopped. "What are you talking about?" asked Henry.

"They had the whole dock closed off until about seven. I wanted to do some early fishing and was told it was off limits. I've rented this space for three years, and that's never happened before."

"We didn't hear about that," said Henry, grabbing Anne's hand and running with her to the parking lot.

"What do we do now?" she asked when they got to the car.

"I don't know if you're game, but I'd like to go to the airport and see if we can get the next plane out to Tamoros."

"You want to land in the middle of an invasion?"

Henry's eyes lit up. "My God, what a story that would be."

"You sound just like Bolivia."

"I'll tell you what," said Henry. "Go to the airport with me, and then you can drive my car back to Miami."

Anne felt as if she was chickening out. But it wasn't her invasion, was it? And she wasn't the one who wanted to be assigned to Beirut. She'd go home, call Jack, and maybe together they could find out what happened to Sandy. Her two best friends disappearing in one week was a little too much.

When they got to the airport they were told that all flights to Tamoros had been canceled.

"I'd be interested in knowing why," Henry told the ticket agent.

"I don't know, sir."

Henry took out his press card and held it under the agent's nose. "I'd like to see the manager."

The agent made a telephone call but before it was finished, Anne spotted some security police coming in their direction and nudged him. "I think we'd better get out of here."

"They can't do anything," said Henry.

"I mean it. They won't know it's us until they get over here."

They casually walked away, as though on their way to board a plane. As soon as they were out the door they headed for the parking lot at a run.

Once out of the parking lot Henry said, "As far as I'm concerned, that just confirmed it."

"They know what paper you were with."

"I don't care what they say," said Henry. "We've still got a free press in this country."

# Betrayed

He picked up the car phone and punched out a number. "Get me Larry," he said, and then waited for a moment. "Larry? Hold the presses. I'm coming in with a headline for Sunday's paper that you're not going to believe."

The fishing boats pulled in close to the beach just before nightfall. Other than some pretty disgusting rations that had been passed out aboard the boat, she hadn't had anything to eat since supper the night before, and she was starving. She was also stiff and sore from sitting on the wooden deck for over twelve hours.

There were only two rubber dinghies per fishing boat, and several trips had to be made to transport all the men to the beach.

Bolivia was eager to be among the first to go, but Tooley held her back. "There's no rush," he said. "The invasion won't start until everyone's there."

"You make it sound like a game."

"In a way it is," he said. "A dangerous game, but still a game."

When they finally got to the beach Bolivia did some stretching exercises on the sand while some of the men ran in place. Tooley just sat down again, and she wondered if he was the type who was chronically lazy.

"What happens next?" she asked him.

"We walk to town."

"*Walk to town?* What kind of invasion is this?"

"There's nothing to invade on this side of the island," said Tooley. "That's why we landed here."

"We're just going to walk to town."

"We'll be passing by small villages on the way, and we're hoping to enlist the people's help. With any luck, it should be a full-fledged uprising by the time we hit the capitol."

"This sounds like a half-baked plan to me," said Bolivia. "Why not just drop a bomb on the capitol?"

"Because this is supposed to look like a spontaneous uprising."

"You mean it's not supposed to look like the Americans are involved."

"Now you're getting the picture," said Tooley.

"Which is why you don't want me in the front."

"Why I don't want either of us in the front."

"And the Tamoron army is just going to sit still for this?"

"We're hoping they'll all be in bed by the time we get there. Of course, Saturday night and all, we could be wrong."

"It wouldn't be an invasion without a little fighting," said Bolivia.

"Bloodthirsty, aren't you?"

"I'd just like to see a little action, that's all."

At a command in Spanish from someone farther up the beach, the men started to get into formation. Bolivia tried to move up, but Tooley dragged her back.

"Remember your promise," he warned her.

She didn't give him an argument. When they got closer to town she would manage to separate herself from him. In the meantime, though, "I want a gun," she told Tooley.

"No gun."

"I'm the only one without one."

He put his arm around her shoulders as if she were one of his buddies. "You don't need one. I'll protect you."

She felt like shrugging off his arm, only it felt good where it was. "What if we get separated?"

"I'll make sure we don't."

"What if you get killed and the Tamoron army captures me and someone tries to rape me?"

"If that happens, take my gun."

"I really hate you, Tooley!"

"I love you too, honey—just stay close."

In large type that took up half the front page, the headline was to read: Invasion of Tamoros? The question mark was just in case he was wrong. If he was, Henry would put the blame on Bolivia.

## Chapter 13

*She was part of the liberation army marching into town. From tall office buildings people were throwing confetti down on their heads, while roars of approval came from the crowds lining both sides of the street. Handsome men with dark eyes ran up to her and pressed roses into her arms; women begged for a chance to kneel down and kiss her feet; children wanted to walk beside her, holding her hand. It was heady stuff, but Bolivia was up to it.*

*Then some of the members of the liberating army hoisted her up so that she was held high in the air, and the throngs cheered her. They began chanting, "Bolivia Smith, Bolivia Smith for El Presidente." It was an honor, of course, but one she would have to turn down. Tamoros might need her, but the* Miami Times *needed her more. She would turn it down with the sure knowledge that every known journalism award would soon be hers.*

*She looked down from the exalted heights and saw Tooley gazing up at her with wide-eye admiration. "I love you," he shouted to her. "You're the bravest, most beautiful woman in the world." Of course he loved her, just as everyone in the crowd loved her. She would say a fond farewell to him and then give him a mention in her article. Redheaded soldiers of fortune who made inventive love in broom closets were fine for a fling, but for the long haul she would concentrate on her career.*

Hey, Bolivia, try to keep up," said Tooley, nudging her in the side.

"I am keeping up," she told him.

"You were practically standing still there for a moment. We can't afford to take rest periods."

"You starve me, you torture me, and then you—"

Tooley's laughter cut her short. "Are you always this dramatic?"

She tried to get back into her fantasy, but she couldn't seem to summon it again. The road was unpaved, and she found that she had to walk with her head down to avoid stepping in holes. The weather was an improvement over Miami, though, with a pleasant breeze coming in off the ocean. She moved along with what she hoped was a manly stride, bringing up the rear of the long column that snaked along the curving road. Occasionally, in the distance, she could see clusters of tiny houses—not much more than shacks, really—up against the hills. An occasional goat or donkey was feeding by the side of the road. Bolivia had never favored rural areas and wished they'd get to the town soon. She was ready for some action, and that was where it would be.

Tooley put his arm around her shoulders in a comradely gesture. He leaned over and whispered in her ear, "We could always take a break behind some bushes for a quickie."

She simultaneously shrugged off his arm and sent her elbow into his ribs.

"What was that for?" he grumbled.

"We're liberating a country, not going on a picnic."

"Who are you, Ernest Hemingway?"

Maybe, and the bell was tolling for her.

"You think you are, don't you?" said Tooley. "You think you're some macho journalist whose mission is to seek out wars and write about them."

"At least I don't take money to fight other people's wars."

"How do you know I'm getting paid?"

"Somehow, Tooley, I don't get the idea that you do things out of the goodness of your heart or the courage of your convictions."

"Is your writing as clichéd as your speech?"

She tried walking faster in an effort to lose him. She was two steps ahead of him when they rounded a bend in the road and came upon a small village. The people were coming out of their houses to see what was happening, and then someone must have told them, because a few cheers were heard.

The men in the village grabbed up the nearest things at hand—machetes, pitchforks, in one case a shovel—and joined them in the march. Several barefoot women in shapeless cotton dresses brought out food and water to hand to the soldiers as they passed. Bolivia accepted a cup of water from a woman who then ran along beside her while she emptied the cup. She heard young boys begging their mothers to be allowed to come along, and some of them were given permission. It would be something to remember and talk about for the rest of their lives.

Excited, Bolivia turned to Tooley. "Isn't this wonderful?"

"Don't get too involved, Bolivia. This isn't your war."

It felt like it. It was the only one she had known firsthand. "Aren't you excited?" she asked him.

"I've got a blister on my left heel, this rifle feels like it weighs a ton, and I'd give a hundred dollars for a cold beer. Does that answer your question?"

"I'll carry the rifle for you."

"No thank you."

"But aren't you the least bit excited?"

"No."

"God, you're cynical. How many wars have you been in, or don't you even remember?"

"This isn't a war, Bolivia, it's just a small invasion. If things go right, we won't even see any fighting."

"Be a spoilsport!"

"You're begging for a fight, aren't you? You fought me, now you want to fight the Tamoron army."

"If you don't enjoy it, I don't see why you do it."

He grinned at her. "The pay is great."

"I knew it," she muttered, trying to distance herself from him. She would never understand how she could be so attracted to a soldier of fortune.

Twenty minutes later they passed through the second village, and word must have reached the inhabitants, because at least four dozen men were waiting to join them. Again they were offered food and drink, and this time Bolivia took a piece of fruit. Tooley warned her to remove the skin first, but she ignored him.

"You drink the water, you eat unwashed fruit, you're going to get sick."

"Quit raining on my parade, Tooley."

"Another original saying. Can I write that down, Bolivia? Are you sure they really pay you to write for a newspaper?"

"I'm a damn good writer."

Tooley was noticeably silent.

"And after this, I'll be a great writer."

"You think this is going to make your career, huh?"

"I know it will."

"Well, enjoy the parade while it lasts, honey."

Somehow, in his mouth, endearments sounded like four letter words.

The sun was setting as they reached the outskirts of Santa Lucia, the capital city, and the lights from the city lit the sky. Before they hit the suburbs they passed through what looked like a shantytown. People were living in cardboard houses or shelters made from tin. There were starving, defeated looking dogs and children with extended stomachs. Bolivia hoped the invasion would change all that.

The march paused here and, up ahead, Bolivia could see some of the men talking to the people. "Stay here," Tooley told her. "I'm going to see what's happening."

She waited until he had gone, then followed behind him keeping to the edge of the road. She was almost up to the head of the troops when someone reached out and grabbed her arm.

She turned and saw Mason grinning at her. "How're you doing?" he asked her.

"Why are we stopping?"

"I hear we're splitting up. One group's going to the presidential palace to arrest the generals, one's going to the radio station to announce the coup, and the rest of the men are supposed to maintain order in the streets. Take my advice and don't volunteer for the last one. The Tamorons tell me that most of the army is downtown on Saturday nights getting drunk. If there's any fighting, that's where it'll be."

"Mason, could you get me a rifle?"

"Sorry, Bolivia."

"Am I just supposed to go in there unprotected?"

"Complain to Tooley about it, not me. Anyway, all I have is my own rifle."

Bolivia reached for her back pocket and felt that her wallet was still there. She pulled it out and removed a twenty-dollar bill, thinking maybe she could buy a weapon from one of the peasants. Money in hand, she started looking around and had just spotted a young boy with a shotgun when someone grabbed her and spun her around.

"What's with the money?" asked Tooley.

Bolivia shoved it back in her pocket.

"Come on," he said. "We're going to the radio station."

"I don't want to go to the radio station. That's the easiest job of all."

"And the only one where you might be of some use," said Tooley. "Newspaper people are supposed to know something about communications."

She had an idea of making a run for it, but he had her by the wrist now and wasn't letting go. "Pay attention to me," he said to her. "We're going to be with a group of Tamorons, and one of them is their leader in exile, Eduardo Centavo. Don't open your mouth to them and don't give me any trouble. *¿Comprende?*"

"Yes," she muttered, finally managing to get her wrist free of him. If he wasn't tying her up, he was holding on to her. She was really getting tired of it.

Groups of men began to disperse down different streets, all leading to the center of town. Tooley and Bolivia towered over their group, most of the Tamorons being small. Of course, Tooley probably towered over everyone, no matter where he was.

The closer they got to town, the more people were seen on the streets. Most of them were headed for downtown, but some of them were standing in clusters talking. Some of them recognized Eduardo Centavo and called to him, and as more and more people saw him, Bolivia could feel the excitement permeating the air. Señor Centavo would only be on the island for one reason, and they seemed to know that.

The Tamoron beside Tooley pointed to a building up ahead, and Bolivia looked up to see the radio tower in the sky. She kept expecting some kind of resistance, but so far everyone seemed to be on their side. Luckily, they hadn't run into any members of the Tamoron army.

Taking over the radio station proved to be so easy that Bolivia knew she was going to have to fictionalize it for her newspaper report. They were profusely welcomed, the men in charge of the station practically falling all over Centavo in their enthusiasm. The group went upstairs to where the broadcast booth was, leaving two men as guards down below.

"What do we do now?" Bolivia asked Tooley. She had expected them to take over for the disc jockey who, with a big smile on his face, was still playing records.

"We wait," said Tooley.

"For what?"

"For a phone call."

"Isn't anyone going to talk into the microphone?"

"Be patient, Bolivia. Nothing happens instantaneously. When we get the call from the presidential palace, then you'll see something happen."

Bolivia went over to the window and looked down at the city. She had a clear view of a large plaza. It seemed filled with people and then she noticed that a group of musicians were playing in the bandstand. People were walking arm in arm around the plaza, and some younger couples were dancing to the music. One minute it looked like a picture postcard setting, and the next she saw flashes of light and then saw the people scattering.

"They're fighting down there," she told Tooley, and he came over to stand beside her.

He opened the window and pushed it out, and now she could hear the sound of sporadic gunfire. "Just some skirmishes," he said. "The army isn't expected to put up much of a fight. It's the secret police we have to worry about, and most of them should be at the palace."

The phone rang, and Centavo picked it up. A few moments later he was taking the place of the disc jockey and speaking into the microphone. He announced to the people that a coup had been effected, that the generals were under house arrest and that there would now be a return to democracy. Then the disc jockey started broadcasting the Tamoron national anthem. It was a plaintive little tune with corny lyrics and a three/four beat that made it sound to Bolivia like a country-western song.

"Is that all there is to it?" she asked Tooley.

"You feeling let down?"

"But it was so easy."

"I knew it," he said.

"You knew what?"

"I knew you wouldn't be happy unless I got killed and you could appropriate my rifle."

"I just thought there'd be more to it. Why did you have to train the men if you didn't think there would be any resistance?"

"There was always the possibility. Anyway, guys get into that kind of training."

Meaning himself, too, she was sure.

"Come on," he said, taking her hand. "Let's go down to the plaza and celebrate."

"I want to phone in my story first," said Bolivia.

"Not yet," said Tooley. "Give them an hour to get this straightened away, and then you can do it. Anyway, the telephone lines are all down until we tell them to start operating again."

"You sure?" she asked him.

"Absolutely. That call you just saw is the last one until we give the go-ahead."

It seemed more like an event when they got down to the street. The energy in the air was palpable. They walked over to the plaza, where everyone was now dancing in celebration, and Bolivia saw soldiers from the Tamoron army toasting each other. If they were as unconcerned as they looked about who was in power, she wondered how the generals had ever taken control. Maybe, like Tooley, these men just liked carrying guns and getting paid and didn't care who did the paying.

Tooley bought them each a rum and Coke, which they quickly drank, and then he pulled her into the center of the plaza. "Would you mind taking your helmet off?" he asked her.

"Why?"

"Because I want to dance with you, and you look like a guy."

Bolivia took it off and handed it to a small boy who was watching her. He quickly put it on his head and ran off, yelling with delight.

Tooley put his arms around her, and they began two-stepping around the plaza. People were looking at them and smiling, and some of the men patted Tooley on the back.

"We really did it," said Bolivia.

"We did."

"We liberated an entire country."

"Well, a small country."

"But we did it." She was starting to feel the excitement she had expected to feel, and she didn't know whether it was the rum or the coup. "This was fun," she said. "Let's liberate another country."

"Any particular one you have in mind?"

"Canada."

"I don't think Canada needs liberating."

"Then let's conquer it!"

Tooley pulled away a little and looked down at her. "I think you're drunk."

"Not on one rum."

"I think you are," he said, his grin coming into play. "Let's have another."

They each downed another and then he said, "Do you want to get something to eat?"

"No, I'm feeling too good."

"How good?"

Bolivia could feel her mouth stretching into an enormous smile as she looked around at all the people. Because of her they were free. Because of her democracy was restored to Tamoros. "Let's dance," she said.

"I have a better idea," said Tooley.

"Well, yes, so do I, but I don't see a broom closet around."

"No, but the Intercontinental is across the plaza. I'll bet they'd rent us a broom closet. Or even a room."

"Heaven," said Bolivia, "is a real bed."

"And a shower with hot water."

"And room service!"

"And a decent night's sleep."

"Don't count on that," she said, feeling more lusty by the moment. It was either war or rum or a combination of both, but she couldn't conceive of doing anything as prosaic as using the bed for sleeping. Not with Tooley around.

They crossed over to the hotel and walked into the lobby. Tooley had some cash on him, but no credit cards, so Bolivia gave her credit card to the desk clerk. It was a silly, sentimental thing, but she wanted the receipt as a souvenir.

It turned out to be a rather second-rate hotel room, but it looked glorious to her. She quickly availed herself of the bathroom, and when she came out, Tooley had opened the sliding glass doors to the balcony and was standing outside. From somewhere he had gotten a bottle of wine, and as she joined him, he was just raising it to his mouth. He passed it to her, and she took a swig before passing it back. That was enough, though; any more and she might not be in any shape to enjoy what was coming next.

Below them the plaza had taken on the appearance of a fiesta. It looked as if most of the population of the island had converged on it, and people were laughing and dancing and hugging each other.

# Betrayed

"I feel just like a queen looking down on my subjects," said Bolivia, feeling very protective of the people below. "Isn't it great to make that many people happy?"

"The generals probably aren't so happy," said Tooley, but the thought didn't seem to bother him.

"I'm happy. This is probably the most exciting day of my life," she said, hoping it would get even more exciting very quickly. Although, if it was even half as exciting as the broom closet had been, she'd be satisfied.

"And it's not over yet," said Tooley, unspoken promises in his voice.

Bolivia turned to him and lifted her face. For a fleeting moment she was sorry there wasn't a movie camera to record the moment: the happy couple on the balcony, the happy throngs below. And then his lips were touching hers, and she lost herself in the kiss.

Which was over awfully quickly. She opened her eyes and gave him a questioning look.

"Excuse me for a moment, okay?" he asked, then went inside.

She surmised he was using the bathroom. She savored the moment, savored what she was sure was going to come next. Then she decided to close the curtains and wait for him in bed.

As she turned to go into the room, she saw him seated on the bed using the telephone. She didn't know whether she was more angry at the fact he had excused himself at such a moment to make a phone call, or whether it was because he had lied about the phones being out of order.

She stepped into the room and, closing the door to drown out the noise of the crowd, she heard him say, "Yes, I'll hold."

"I thought you said they didn't work?" she said.

"It just works inside the hotel," he said.

"Who are you calling?"

He put his hand over the mouthpiece. "Would you mind waiting outside for a minute, Bolivia?" He gave her such a warm, loving smile she was instantly suspicious.

She tried to make a joke of it. "What is it? Did you have a date tonight you have to break?"

He started to chuckle, seemed about to speak and reassure her, but then he said into the phone, "A telex downstairs? Great, I'll be down as soon as I complete my call. And do me a favor, don't let anyone else get to it first."

Bolivia crossed her arms. "What's going on, Tooley?"

"Nothing, sweetheart. How about being a good girl and waiting outside for me?"

Bolivia didn't quite see red, but it was pretty close. "Why do you need a telex?"

Tooley's body language was suddenly signaling that he was about to step on broken glass. "I'll explain it later. I don't have time right now."

"You'll explain it *now*."

And then he was saying into the phone, "Jeff, it's Tooley. Now take down every word of this. Tonight, at ten o'clock—"

In a swift, decisive move, Bolivia yanked the telephone cord out of the wall.

Looking furious, Tooley yelled, "What in hell did you do that for?"

"What are you trying to do, ruin my exclusive? Did you think you could make a few bucks by calling it in yourself? Of all the low, rotten tricks to pull on me, this is the lowest!"

A pause. "Time to wake up, Bolivia."

"I ought to throw you off the balcony for that little trick. You'll do anything for money, won't you? You're nothing but a male prostitute!"

"Did you really think I was undercover all that time because I was gung ho to carry a gun?"

"No, I figured you were getting paid."

His smile was mocking. "I get paid by the New York *Tribune*."

It was like a blow to the stomach. "Why you sneaky, conniving—"

"Reporter. Just like you."

"You're still not beating me out of my exclusive!"

"Honey, I got there first. I'm sure you'll be able to do a nice follow-up for your paper. Just look at it this way: If it weren't for me, you wouldn't have been able to come along."

"If it weren't for you, I wouldn't have been tied up and gagged. If you think you're going to get away with this, you—" She hauled off to slug him, but in a quick move he caught her fist and twisted her arm behind her, and the next thing she knew, like déjà vu, she found her wrists secured by his scarf.

"Now, don't get upset, honey," he said, trying to hold her still while she kicked out at him.

"If you don't untie me this second, Tooley—"

"I'm going to lock you in the room while I go downstairs, then I'll be back and we'll talk things over."

"We have nothing to talk over, you traitor!"

"Hey, you would have done the same thing."

"I wouldn't have made love to you in a broom closet!"

"That had nothing to do with this."

She wanted to spit at him, but her mouth was too dry. "Every move you've made had something to do with this. You've lied to me about everything."

He grinned. "Well, almost everything."

"You dirty, rotten—"

"Be reasonable, Bolivia. I couldn't risk your blowing my cover. Now be good. I'll be right back."

He pushed her aside as he headed for the door. No sooner had the door closed than she heard the key turning in the lock on the other side.

Like hell he was going to beat her to an exclusive. Damn the New York *Tribune*. She had always hated that paper, anyway.

She went over to the telephone and, using her shoulders, knocked it to the floor. Taking careful aim with her toe, she kicked it with all her force up and through the glass door. It was the best placekick she had ever made and she didn't care that her toe felt as if she'd just broken it. He was very wrong if he thought he could keep her prisoner this time.

Backing to the broken door, she moved the scarf binding her wrists down to a jagged piece of glass. Moments later her wrists were free.

She went out onto the balcony and looked down. She was three floors up, too high to jump. But there was a balcony right below hers. She climbed over the railing, then swung her body so that when she fell she'd land on the next balcony. From that balcony she jumped to the street. Her feet were already so numb from the long march that she barely felt it when she landed.

She ran back into the lobby and asked the clerk where the telex machine was located. He pointed to an office behind him, and she raced in and saw Tooley just getting set up on the machine.

He didn't see her, but she saw an old, manual typewriter sitting on a desk. She picked it up, and before he

## Betrayed

knew what was happening she sent it smashing down on the telex machine, completely demolishing it.

"What the hell?" Tooley shouted, getting up. He started to head for the phone on the desk, and, as he did, she picked up the wooden chair he had been sitting in and brought it down on his head.

With a great sense of satisfaction, she watched him slowly crumple to the ground. She checked his pulse to make sure she hadn't committed murder—although she was feeling more than a little murderous toward him—and then tore the telephone out of the wall before racing out of the hotel.

She ran two blocks before slowing down to a walk. She had to find a telephone, but she also had to change her appearance. Tooley would come to, and when he did, he'd be looking for her. And he'd have all the other men looking for her, too.

She walked by a store for tourists, then stopped and went back. Availing herself once more of her credit card, she emerged from the store three minutes later in cotton shorts, rubber thongs, a T-shirt that had a map of Tamoros on it and a straw hat. Now she looked like every other tourist on the island.

She entered the next hotel she came to and asked the clerk if they had a telex machine.

"Yes, we do," he said in perfect English. "We also have a Fax machine."

That was good, but not as good as a telephone. "Are the phones working yet?" she asked him.

"The phones were never out of order."

Another lie of Tooley's.

"Will you be checking in?" the clerk asked her.

It seemed safer then making the call down in the lobby where anyone could see her.

"I can't believe you're in the office this late. Henry, have I got a story for you!"

"Where are you, Bolivia?"

She took a deep breath and smiled. "Tamoros."

"Thank God. It's true, then."

"What's true?"

"There was an invasion, right?"

"How could you possibly have known that?"

"We figured it out, Bolivia. Me and your friend Anne."

"You *couldn't* have figured it out."

"We did. I even ran the headline of the invasion for tomorrow's paper. I have a question mark at the end of it, but I can change it in the later editions."

"This really ticks me off, Henry. I get the exclusive of my career, and you beat me to it?"

"All I had was a headline, Bolivia, and some supposition. You'll get your exclusive when you fill in the rest."

"I get tied up, gagged, tortured, and you scoop me! It's not fair."

"It sounds like a great story. Keep talking."

"Can you get me off the island? I can be at the office in a couple of hours and write it myself." And ensure that it was actually going out under her byline.

"I'll hold the presses 'til you get here. Listen, I'll call a friend at the American embassy. Head for there now, and I'll make sure you get out."

"What am I getting out of this, Henry?"

"I'll definitely put in for a raise for you. And your expenses are covered."

"I don't want a raise. I want Beirut."

There was a short silence. "Beirut is no place for a woman."

*Betrayed*

"I just went in with an invasion, Henry. I think I can handle Beirut."

"We'll talk about it when you get here."

"We'll talk about it now or I'll call another newspaper."

"You wouldn't do that."

"Try me."

"Okay, you've got it. You've got Beirut."

"I want it in writing."

"Right now you've got my word for it. I'll have it in writing by the time you get here."

The embassy man drove her to the airport. "This is the last plane going out to the States," he told her, "until we're sure the situation is resolved here."

"I appreciate it," said Bolivia.

"Although if you wanted to stay on and finish your vacation, I think I can assure you that you'll be in no danger."

From the start he had assumed she was a tourist, and she hadn't disabused him of the notion. He probably thought she was one of Henry's girlfriends.

"No, I think I'd like to go back," she said.

"All the excitement scared you, did it? But you'll soon be safe and sound at home."

She felt like tying him up and gagging him.

She wasn't the only one at the airport trying to get out; it was full of tourists. The embassy man secured her ticket, then walked her over to the boarding area. "You'll be okay on your own?" he asked her. "It's boarding in just a minute."

"I'll be fine," Bolivia assured him.

"Say hi to Henry for me."

"Don't worry, I will. And thanks."

Bolivia spotted a candy bar machine and was heading for it when she saw him. He hadn't seen her yet, but he was hard to miss. The combat gear was noticeable enough, but so was the lump on the top of his red head. She almost laughed out loud at the sight until she realized she still hadn't given the story to Henry, and if Tooley saw her he'd probably stop that from happening. And he was heading for the boarding area, which meant he also had a ticket on the last flight out.

Just as she heard her flight being called she saw two airport security police coming out of a door into the terminal. She put what she hoped was a panicked expression on her face and then ran over to them, her chest heaving with phony sobs.

"Help, help," she said to them in English. "That man over there, that man..."

"What happened? What is it?" one of them asked her, his English almost fluent.

She looked down, feigning embarrassment. "The big man. The one with the red hair."

"The soldier?"

She nodded, wiping at her eyes.

"What happened, miss?"

"He...He... He opened his pants and...and... exposed himself to me."

"They think they can do what they want in our country," one of the men said to the other in Spanish.

"Arrogant American," said the other. "Let's teach him a lesson before he tries the same thing on one of our women."

They walked on either side of her over to the boarding area, where people were already getting on the plane. Tooley saw her then and did the stupidest thing he could have chosen to do. He gave her his wicked grin, and the security men, seeing it, rushed up to him and pulled their guns.

As Bolivia got to the top of the boarding steps, she turned around and saw Tooley being led through the door the men had emerged from. With no ID on him, he could be a while. And in the meantime, she'd be in Miami filing her story.

Oh, yes—revenge was sweet!

## Chapter 14

"Good evening. I'm Ned Copper, and this is *Newsline*."

A film clip was shown of the island of Tamoros as a voice-over gave details of the invasion. An elated Eduardo Centavo was seen hugging Tooley, the message unstated but clear: Tooley had been one of those responsible for overthrowing the military dictatorship. "We have with us tonight," said Ned, "in our New York office, the intrepid reporter from the *New York Tribune*, the man who went undercover as a member of the invading forces, my old friend and colleague, Jim O'Toole. Nice to have you with us, Tooley."

"Nice to be here, Ned."

"And from Tamoros, in his first televised interview since the coup, Señor Eduardo Centavo. Good of you to take the time to be with us, Señor Centavo."

"Thank you, Ned."

The camera zoomed in for a close-up of Tooley as Ned was heard asking, "How in the world did you do it, Tooley?"

Tooley was ostentatiously wearing combat fatigues, as though still living in the jungle and not in New York City. Bolivia saw the familiar grin, the familiar gleam in his not-to-be-trusted green eyes, and immediately saw red.

This should have been *her* interview. Granted, her story hadn't appeared until Monday's paper, but neither had Tooley's. And the *Times* had been the only paper to break the story on Sunday. In her opinion the story of a female reporter, taken prisoner and then becoming part of the invasion, was far more interesting than a reporter who had gone undercover just to get a story.

Halfway into Tooley's narration, Ned interrupted with, "What about this female reporter, the one from the *Times*? What was she like?"

Tooley's perennial grin faded a bit as he shook his head a little. "Let me put it to you this way, Ned. We've both run into the type of female reporter who thinks combat zones should be air-conditioned and have running hot and cold..." He let his words trail off as the camera panned to Ned, one eyebrow raised, obviously not wanting to be put in the position of criticizing female reporters.

"Let's just say," said Tooley, "that she was one big pain in the—"

Bolivia's foot went right through the TV screen, and with an accompanying satisfying sound, Tooley was obliterated from the screen.

Bolivia was feeling such guilt at having stood up Anne and Sandy on Friday that she got to Neiman Marcus early on Tuesday night and was prepared to accept, no complaints, any dress that Anne had decided on.

Anne was even earlier. "You sure look better than the last time I saw you," she said, giving Bolivia a hug as she stepped out of the elevator.

"Surprising what a shower and shampoo will do for you," said Bolivia. "Is Sandy coming?"

"She's meeting us for dinner afterwards."

The dress fit perfectly, and even if she had wanted to complain, she could find nothing to complain about. If she had to wear a dress, this one was about as inoffensive as you could get.

"It sure is plain," she said to Anne, turning around in front of the mirror in order to get a look at the back.

"You think it's too plain?" asked Anne.

"No, it's great. I could have it shortened after the wedding and wear it to work." There were times when a more corporate look was required. She'd had a skirt she wore on such occasions, but the last time she had taken it to be cleaned, it had finally disintegrated in the process. She hadn't mourned its passing.

"What do I wear with it?" asked Bolivia, looking down at her ankles, which still bore the marks of having been bound.

"Flats or sandals. You can coordinate the color with Sandy. She's going to wear heels."

"That's it? Nothing else?"

"Well..."

"Come on, Annie, I'm not going to give you a hard time."

"Sandy and I picked out straw hats."

Bolivia pictured fancy concoctions, at the very least a big picture hat with a trailing ribbon, but when Anne took her down to the first floor and showed her the plain straw bowler, she put it on her head and loved it. It could almost be a man's hat, it had such a jaunty look. After the wedding she'd be able to wear it with her regular clothes.

"Hey, I like it," said Bolivia.

"It looks great on you."

"I was afraid it was going to have flowers or bows."

"Well, I was thinking of a band of flowers just for the wedding, but it could come off afterwards."

"Sure," said Bolivia, and caught Anne's look of relief. "Annie, relax. After what you guys went through to find me, you think I'm going to give you a hard time over a few flowers? If you'd shown me a pink hat with a ruffled veil I wouldn't have objected."

"If I'd known that . . ." said Anne.

"But I'm glad you didn't. This is a great hat." She was all prepared to wear it out of the store until Anne informed her that she'd already purchased the hats on Friday.

At first Bolivia had been a little upset with Henry and Anne for having beaten her with the headline, but after Tooley got his story in as fast as she did, she was glad they'd done it. Tooley probably couldn't believe how soon the *Times* had headlined the invasion. He was probably still trying to figure out how she could have sneaked off and found a phone without his being aware of it.

Sandy was waiting for them inside the restaurant. Bolivia had talked to her since she'd been back but hadn't seen her, and now she asked, "How's it going?"

Sandy said, "You ought to see how nice they're being to me after locking me up."

"As well they ought," said Anne.

"It wasn't the lieutenant's fault," said Sandy. "We're always being forced to cooperate with the government whether we want to or not."

They were led to a table, and they ordered drinks before Sandy said, "Come on, Bolivia, we want to hear about it."

"You read my article, didn't you?"

"Not about the invasion," said Sandy. "About the redhead you ran off with."

"That seems to be a touchy subject with her," said Anne. "I asked her on Sunday, and she almost bit my head off."

"I figured you'd eloped with him," said Sandy.

Bolivia took a deep breath to calm herself down. It didn't work. "If you're talking about that lying piece of scum Tooley—"

"Hey, tone it down," said Anne. "You've now got the attention of the entire restaurant."

Bolivia glanced around and saw that her friend was right. She lowered her voice and said, "You want to know what that sonuvabitch did to me? You ready for this?"

Anne and Sandy looked enthralled.

"He had the gall to tie me up and gag me!"

Anne's mouth fell open, but Sandy, if Bolivia was reading her correctly, was trying not to smile. "What's so funny?" she asked.

"He actually gagged you?" asked Sandy, sounding all choked up, but it wasn't from sympathy.

"Every time I opened my mouth, it seemed like he was putting a gag in it again."

"I would've given him a good, swift kick," said Anne.

"I did. I also spat at him."

Sandy had her napkin up to her face, and her eyes were tearing.

"I fail to see what's amusing you," said Bolivia.

"I don't know—it just seems funny."

"Well, it wasn't," said Bolivia, thinking she wasn't getting the proper support from her friends. But then Sandy always did have a weird way of looking at things.

"Well, too bad," said Anne. "I really thought you were finally attracted to a man."

"Oh, I was attracted," said Bolivia.

"To a man who tied you up and gagged you?"

Sandy was now laughing openly.

Bolivia shrugged. "I wasn't tied and gagged all the time. And we did have some good fights."

Sandy and Anne exchanged a knowing look.

"Okay, so I like to fight with men. What's the matter with that?"

"Nothing," said Anne.

"Perfectly normal behavior," said Sandy.

"Also, I asked for it. I mean, I could've cooperated, but I didn't. I was given a choice, but at the time I preferred being gagged to cooperating."

"Of course," said Anne.

"Makes perfect sense," said Sandy, rolling her eyes.

"You think I'm nuts, don't you?"

"Was that it?" said Sandy. "Just fighting all the time? Didn't he even kiss you?"

"Let's order," said Bolivia. "I'm starved."

"She thinks she's being subtle," Anne said.

"Evading the issue," agreed Sandy.

"Listen, do I ask you personal questions?"

"All the time," said Anne, and Sandy nodded in agreement.

Bolivia lowered her voice. "Well, there was this broom closet aboard the ship..."

Anne looked amazed. "A *broom* closet?"

"Exactly what I said," said Bolivia.

"And...?"

Bolivia smiled.

"You didn't!" said Sandy.

"Oh, I don't believe it!" Anne hooted.

Bolivia felt a little smug as she said, "Believe it!"

The waiter came with their drinks and asked for their order, and Bolivia could tell that the others were dying to hear the details. Well, they could fill them in for themselves—they had imaginations.

Anyhow, she didn't want to talk about that aspect of her relationship with Tooley. She kept dreaming about him at night and waking up in a cold sweat. It would start off with them making love, and everything would be wonderful, but it always ended with them at each other's throats and a gag in her mouth. The dreams pretty much indicated her mixed feelings about him, but she'd just as soon not be so vividly reminded.

As soon as the waiter left Sandy said, "Are you in love with him?"

"Are you kidding? I hate his guts."

"She's in love with him," said Anne.

"No way," said Bolivia. "Me in love with some hotshot *Tribune* reporter who lied to me from square one? No way. Whatever it was, it wasn't love."

"Wait a minute," said Sandy. "I don't get it. You liked him when you thought he was a vet in a wheelchair, but you don't like him as a reporter for the *Tribune*? That doesn't make any sense."

"I liked him in spite of being a vet, and in spite of being in a wheelchair," said Bolivia. "But just another guy out for a story? No thanks. You know what he did to me at the end? He tied me up and locked me in the hotel room so that he could beat me to an exclusive. Can you believe that?"

Sandy and Anne exchanged looks again.

"You would've done the same thing to him," said Sandy.

"Without a qualm," said Anne.

"That's not the point," said Bolivia. "The point is, *he* did it to *me*."

"And that was the end of it?" asked Sandy.

"Not quite," said Bolivia. "I got loose, went downstairs and found the lying bastard using the telex. So I broke a chair over his head."

"Oh, dear," said Anne. "It sounds like true love to me."

"You're lucky you didn't kill him," said Sandy, who was big on law and order.

"*He* was lucky," said Bolivia.

"That was it?" asked Anne. "You left him for dead and flew back to Miami?"

"You're lucky you're not in jail over there," said Sandy.

"He's lucky *he* isn't," said Bolivia, then told them about accusing Tooley of exposing himself at the airport.

"I don't know, Annie," said Sandy, "but I'm beginning to wonder why we were worried about her. It seems like I spent twenty-four hours locked up just so she could create mayhem in Tamoros."

"And I gave up my Saturday with Jack."

"Mayhem? *Mayhem?* He deserved every bit of it!"

"I don't suppose he's called you since you've been back," said Anne.

"He wouldn't dare. I'd hang up on him."

Another look was exchanged between them, and Bolivia asked, "Will you stop it? Do you two really believe I'm just dying to have him call?"

"It sounds like you have a lot in common," said Sandy.

"I don't want to talk about it anymore," said Bolivia. "Anyway, I've got some good news to tell you."

"Oh, no," said Anne.

"What?" said Bolivia.

"Henry said you asked for Beirut. Don't tell me he agreed."

"I've got it in writing," said Bolivia. "But don't worry, I won't miss your wedding. I don't go until the first of September."

"I wasn't worried about my wedding," said Anne.

Sandy looked stricken. "I can't believe I'm losing my two best friends!"

Anne said, "I'm getting married, Sandy, not going to Beirut."

Bolivia looked around the table. "Isn't anyone going to congratulate me?"

"That's like congratulating you for jumping off a bridge," said Anne.

"You're going to end up a hostage," said Sandy, "and it's not going to be as fun as it was with Tooley."

"Anyone tries to take *me* hostage, they better watch out," said Bolivia.

"Before I forget," said Anne, "we're going to have an informal wedding rehearsal at Jack's house on Friday night. Plan on eating with us, too."

"What about a bachelor party?" asked Sandy. "Are the three of us going out Saturday night?"

"Let's hit all the bars and really tie one on," said Bolivia.

Anne shook her head. "I've got something better in mind, but it's going to be a surprise."

It should have been the greatest week of Bolivia's life. After her semiexclusive she should have been asked to appear on all the talk shows, been interviewed for all the news magazines and generally been feted as the reporter of the year. Instead, everywhere she looked she saw Tooley. Just when she was congratulating herself that she'd gone a whole couple of hours without even thinking about him, she would walk into a drugstore and see him on the cover of some magazine. Or walk into a bar and see him holding forth on a talk show.

She was a minor celebrity in Miami for a couple of days, but Miami wasn't the whole country. She was asked to speak to a Tamoron refugee group, but when she showed up they all wanted to know about Tooley. He seemed to be some sort of folk hero to them, and she was only a poor substitute. It turned out that some of the people working at her hotel were Tamorons, but that didn't get her any air-conditioning.

A couple of times she picked up her phone and almost called Tooley just to chew him out. Then she remembered his remarks about her on TV and slammed it back down. September first couldn't come fast enough as far as she was concerned. Putting several thousand miles between herself and Tooley was just what was needed.

The week seemed to drag, and she actually started to look forward to the wedding. After the excitement of the previous week, the ordinary things, like softball games and writing her column, seemed mundane.

And dreams of Tooley were still driving her up the wall at night.

Anne's surprise turned out to be all day Saturday and Saturday night for the three of them at a local health spa. Only Anne had ever been to one before, and Sandy and Bolivia didn't know what to expect.

They all enjoyed it.

During the day they swam in the pool and worked on their tans and were served minuscule meals that must have been healthy because they sure weren't filling. They were massaged and saunaed. They were given a leg wax and a bikini wax. They were left in a steam room for an hour and then given facials. Their hair was shampooed and conditioned, and Sandy opted for a haircut. Bolivia had a slight trim, and Anne had a few streaks put in her already sun-streaked hair.

Bolivia sneaked out for a brief period that evening and sneaked back in with a bottle of champagne. When she got back Anne and Sandy were getting manicures and pedicures, and Bolivia went along with everything but the polish. Then they retired to their suite and toasted Anne on the end of her freedom.

They got sentimental and nostalgic, all of them realizing that something was coming to an end. The three musketeers were now one down and two to go.

"I guess it had to happen eventually," said Sandy, who was showing the effects of the champagne more than the others. "I'll miss you guys, though. I really will."

"I keep telling you, I'm not going anywhere," said Anne.

"Yeah, but it'll be different."

"You guys can visit me in Beirut," said Bolivia, but got groans in answer.

"It's even changing at work," said Sandy. "Did I tell you I got a new partner?"

"Did she tell us that?" Anne asked Bolivia.

"I think she neglected that little fact," said Bolivia.

"But she always tells us everything."

"Then there must be a very good reason why we haven't heard about it."

"I invited him to the wedding tomorrow," said Sandy. "I hope that's okay."

"Are we supposed to bring *dates*?" asked Bolivia.

"Of course not," said Anne. "But you're welcome to if you want."

"I don't want to bring a date," said Bolivia.

"His name is Chance," said Sandy.

They both looked at her.

"Chance Madrigal."

"That's a really pretty name," said Anne.

"If you think the *name's* pretty," said Sandy, "wait until you see *him*."

Bolivia and Anne exchanged glances.

"That good?" asked Anne.

Sandy gave them a smug smile. "Better."

"Well, well," said Bolivia. "And you're the one complaining about things changing?"

"Is he married?" asked Anne.

"No."

"Don't you get married, too," said Bolivia, thinking she was going to end up with all married friends and have no one to go out drinking with when she came back to town.

"I'm not even sure I like him," said Sandy.

"Well, don't worry," said Anne. "We'll check him out for you at the wedding."

"Don't do anything without our approval," said Bolivia.

Sandy started to cry.

"Hey, if he's that bad, don't bring him to the wedding," said Bolivia. "And ask for a different partner."

"I'm not crying about Chance," said Sandy. "I'm crying because I'm so happy for Annie. She's going to be such a beautiful bride, and we're going to ruin her wedding in those plain dresses. I'm sorry we refused to wear pink, Annie."

Anne smiled. "Oh, I never intended to have those pink dresses," she said. "I just brought out that picture first so you wouldn't complain when I sprang the real ones on you."

"Shall we kill her now or later?" asked Bolivia.

"Right now," said Sandy, lifting a pillow off her bed.

Bolivia guessed it was a perfect day for a wedding, if ninety-eight degrees and ninety-eight percent humidity made for perfection. At least it wasn't raining, and no hurricane warnings were in effect.

They drove from the spa over to Anne's apartment to pick up their clothes, then switched to an Oldsmobile convertible Anne had rented for the honeymoon, and drove to Jack's large Spanish house in Coral Gables.

Jack was getting ready downstairs in the den and left them the master bedroom and bath upstairs to get dressed in.

They heard the doorbell ringing and people arriving almost as soon as they had closed the bedroom door. "How many are coming?" asked Bolivia.

"Quite a few," said Anne. "It kind of got out of hand.

## Betrayed

Jack's friends and relatives, my relatives, the other attorneys where I work, people from the Public Defender's office, our softball team, a few musicians—"

"You invited your old boyfriends?" asked Sandy.

"They're friends of mine," said Anne. "Anyway, that way we have live music for the reception. I also invited Henry, Bolivia. I hope you don't mind."

"You mean my boss Henry?"

"Well, I did spend most of last weekend with him. And Jack and I both like him."

"I hope you didn't invite *my* boss," said Sandy.

Anne looked so gorgeous in her wedding dress and veil that she could have posed for the cover of a magazine. Not that Annie didn't usually look gorgeous, but even Bolivia could see that this was something special. Sandy looked good, too, and instead of looking twelve, the way she did in some of her clothes, she looked like a high school senior going to her prom.

Bolivia wasn't sure how she looked. She was so used to seeing herself in certain kinds of clothes that a long dress came as a shock to her. To make Anne happy she had agreed to a little coral lipstick, but she stood firm when it came to eye makeup. The hat she loved, and the flowers they were to carry were exotic looking and not at all the kind of sweet little posy sort of thing she had expected.

"When do we go down?" asked Bolivia.

"When we hear the music."

"What music?"

Anne gave them a rueful look. "My mother insisted on playing the piano. I, however, vetoed the wedding march. Our signal is *Night Moves*."

"Bob Seger?"

Anne nodded. "If we can recognize my mother's version of it."

When the music started they moved to the head of the stairs. Then Sandy and Bolivia started down. At the bottom of the stairs some guy with a video camera was recording their every move. Bolivia mugged for the camera, and the guy quickly pointed it at Sandy. The stairs ended at the entry hall, where they turned left and walked down the center of the living room, past all the guests on either side. They passed through the arched entryway to the dining room, where the ceremony was to take place.

Jack was already standing beside the judge who was performing the ceremony. The judge nodded to them, and Jack smiled. They positioned themselves and looked out at the people.

Bolivia spotted a Hollywood-handsome hunk in a blue suit and bent down to Sandy's ear. "Get a load of the guy in the blue suit, right behind Annie's brother."

"That's my new partner," said Sandy without moving her lips.

"You wish!"

"It is. That's Chance."

"Well, my advice to you is, take a chance!"

She saw that Sandy was trying not to laugh, and she stopped talking. The last thing she wanted to do was cause them to start breaking up at Annie's wedding.

The telephone started to ring, and Bolivia glanced over at Jack. He shrugged and said, "Let it ring."

After twenty-seven rings, someone Bolivia didn't know moved to the phone and pulled the plug out of the wall.

Pretty soon Bolivia spotted Annie in the entry hall, approaching them fast. Bolivia looked over at Jack and watched the way his face lit up. The only time Bolivia had ever seen Tooley's face light up over her was when he was putting the gag in place. But then, Jack was a sweetheart and Tooley was a dirty, rotten lying—

Anne was taking her place in front of the judge, Jack moving to her side. Bolivia saw them take each other's hand and hold on tightly.

The doorbell rang.

The judge raised an eyebrow at Jack, who nodded for him to begin. Bolivia had her back to the crowd now, but she could hear someone opening the front door, voices, and then a hushed silence as the judge began to speak.

It wasn't any ceremony Bolivia had ever heard of, and she figured Annie must have written it. It had a lot of legalese in it, but it also had some poetry. It was also blessedly brief.

Bolivia didn't cry. She never cried. But when Jack and Anne moved into each other's arms for the kiss at the end, she was feeling pretty emotional. She looked at Sandy and saw tears streaming down her cheeks, which didn't surprise her, as Sandy was the romantic of the bunch.

Then Jack and Annie broke apart and turned around to face the crowd. "Food and drink outside," Anne told everyone, and the people began to move up to offer their congratulations.

It was then that she saw him. Standing at the back, towering over everyone else, was her nemesis himself.

"My God," breathed Sandy beside her. "Is that...?"

Bolivia nodded, her eyes fastened on Tooley. He had shaved his beard, revealing a strong jaw. But the bushy mustache was still in place, as was the long hair tied neatly back.

The crowd seemed to part in front of him, and she took in his cream linen suit, his turquoise silk shirt, the panama hat he held in one hand.

"That's the most incredible looking man I've ever seen," said Sandy. "He looks like he could invade a country single-handedly."

Bolivia felt someone taking her hand and looked down into the eyes of Annie's mother.

"Hi, Mrs. Larkin," she said.

"I haven't seen you in ages, Bolivia. When are you girls going to be getting married?" she asked, including Sandy in her look.

"Well..." said Sandy.

"I'm in no hurry," said Bolivia.

"You girls aren't getting any younger," Mrs. Larkin warned them before moving off.

Bolivia moved over to Annie intending to say, *Excuse me, but I'm taking off,* but Annie grabbed hold of her hand and held on to it.

"Is that Tooley?" she asked, watching his approach.

"I guess it has to be, unless there are two red giants around."

"Who invited him?" asked Bolivia.

"It looks like he's with Henry. Now don't you dare run out of here, Bolivia," she said, knowing Bolivia's reaction exactly. "Anyway, I'd like to meet him."

Tooley was only a couple of feet away now, and Bolivia turned around and fled. There was a tiny powder room off the kitchen, and she went inside and locked the door. She opened the window that looked out over the yard and saw that most of the guests were now outside and lined up to get food and drink.

She heard a knock on the door and froze. "Bolivia, it's me, let me in," said Sandy.

Bolivia turned to the door. "Go away, Sandy, I'm busy."

"You're not going to spend the entire reception locked up in there. Now come out and act like an adult. I want to meet Tooley."

"Then introduce yourself."

"It's Annie's wedding, Bolivia, you can't spoil it."

"I'm not spoiling anything. Just send him away and I'll come out."

She heard some talking outside the door, and then Henry's voice was heard. "I brought a friend of yours along, Bolivia."

"Thanks, Henry, you're a pal."

"He came to the office looking for you, and I told him you were going to be in a wedding. So he came along with me. Nice fellow, real professional. I'm sorry we were late."

"He's about as nice as an attacking cobra, Henry," she said, then her arm was grabbed from behind. She turned to see Tooley at the window, his head and one arm inside.

"Let go of me before I slam down that window and decapitate you," she yelled at him.

He grinned. "I'd like to see you try that, Bolivia. Sorry you didn't manage it with the chair the other night."

"I wish I had!"

"I know you do."

She threw herself back against the door, and he let go of her arm. But now he had both arms through the window and was starting to pull himself inside.

"Get the hell out of here, you bastard!"

He paused halfway in. "And here I was thinking this looked similar to a broom closet."

Bolivia looked around for a weapon, but there was only a box of Kleenex and a dish with scented soap.

"You're looking awfully pretty dressed up like a woman," he said, his eyes wicked.

"What're you supposed to be, Humphrey Bogart in *Casablanca*?"

"I take it you admire my suit."

"I don't admire anything about you, you sneaky, underhanded—"

"I believe they mean the same thing."

Bolivia turned to the sink and ran the water. Then she grabbed up one of the little pink bars of soap that was shaped like a shell and got her hands all soapy.

"What're you doing, Bolivia?"

"This," she said, turning around and slapping her soapy hands against his eyes. She heard a yelp of pain as she opened the bathroom door and ran out.

She went out on the patio, past Tooley, who was standing under the window holding his hands to his eyes. She saw Sandy and her new partner standing by the bar that had been set up and went over to join them in a drink.

Sandy said, "About time," then handed her a glass of champagne.

Bolivia looked back at Tooley and Sandy followed her gaze. "What did you do to him?" asked Sandy.

"Put soap in his eyes."

"Oh, that's so mean," said Sandy, and before Bolivia could stop her, she was heading in Tooley's direction.

"Hi," said Chance to Bolivia.

"Hi."

"I'm Sandy's partner."

"I know."

"You always treat guys like that?"

"Yes."

Bolivia saw Sandy leading Tooley into the kitchen. Motherly Sandy would probably rinse his eyes out for him.

"Nice house," Chance was saying, but Bolivia was already walking away. The softball team was gathered around the food table, and she hardly recognized them in dresses.

"Listen, guys, I need a ride home," she said.

"Sure," said Ginger, "I'll give you a ride."

"Right now."

"Ah, come on, Bolivia, the band hasn't even started playing yet. Annie said she'd introduce us to the musicians."

"Can I borrow your car and come back and pick you up later?"

Ginger sighed. "Bolivia, you're her best friend. You can't just leave in the middle of the reception. Anyway, you might catch the bridal bouquet." This last sentiment was rendered with a big grin.

"I don't care, I've got to get out of here," said Bolivia.

"Going somewhere?" came Tooley's voice from behind her.

She turned around, her hand already raised to throw her champagne at him, but he grabbed her wrist and lowered it so that the champagne spilled on the grass.

"Didn't your parents teach you how to behave in public?" Tooley asked her.

Bolivia glared at him. He was right, though; she couldn't create a scene at Annie's reception.

"Look at me," he said. "A little soap in my eyes, but I'm not mad at you. A lump on the back of my head, an embarrassing moment or two with airport security, but I don't hold a grudge."

She wanted to kick him and dirty those cream linen pants of his, but she held herself in check.

"That was a nice little story you wrote," he said, his grin positively evil.

His pants were a few degrees closer to going to the cleaners.

"Full of clichés, of course, but what can you expect?"

Her hand made a fist without her even thinking about it, and then she took a swing. In a quick move Tooley grabbed her wrist again and forcefully lowered it.

"You can still be tied and gagged, you know," he told her.

"You wouldn't dare!"

"Are you daring me?"

"You don't have the guts!"

Annie stepped into Bolivia's view and ceremoniously removed her veil and handed it to him. "Here, use this to gag her."

Then Sandy was handing him Chance's red and blue striped tie. "You can use this to tie her wrists."

"I don't believe this," said Bolivia, backing away from them and then running to the end of the yard, where it ended at a canal.

Her best friends, aiding and abetting her enemy!

She kicked off her shoes and then sat down on the retaining wall, dangling her legs over the side. She wanted to hit him, and at the same time she wanted to kiss him. She wanted to kill him, and she also wanted to make love to him. It was a hopeless situation any way she looked at it. Why, oh why, had she fallen in love with the man she most wanted to hate?

She didn't even flinch when he sat down next to her. He was going to get grass stains all over his pants, but he

# Betrayed

didn't seem to care. He put his panama hat on his head and stared out over the water.

He said, "The flasher bit was brilliant."

She started to smile. "Did they give you a hard time?"

"Oh, yes. Quite a bit of talk about what I might do to their sisters."

Bolivia chuckled.

"The typewriter on the telex wasn't bad, either."

"I'm glad I didn't kill you," said Bolivia.

"Well, there's still time. I can see you killing me sometime in the future."

"Except I won't be around."

"Well, isn't that a coincidence, neither will I. I'm going to Beirut."

Bolivia turned to him. "Henry told you, didn't he?"

"Yes, but I'd already gotten the assignment."

"You were just going to take off to Beirut? *Alone?*"

"Isn't that what you were going to do?"

She bit her lip and turned away.

"Hey, I was going to take you along with me."

"As what?"

"As my assistant."

Bolivia swung around and glared at him. "It'll be a cold day in hell when I'll be *your* assistant!"

"You really have to concentrate on ridding yourself of those clichés, Bolivia."

She reached out to shove him into the water, but he grabbed her and pulled her down on the grass.

"Let go of me! We're at a wedding reception!"

"That wasn't going to stop you from shoving me in the water."

"Did I ever tell you how much I hated you, Tooley?"

"Yeah, sweetheart, I hate you, too," he said, right before his lips closed over hers.

"Did you see that?" Anne asked Sandy.

"I saw it."

"Watch, though, in another minute they'll be fighting."

Sandy grinned. "I know."

"Did you ever in your life think you'd see Bolivia that crazy about a guy?"

"Never."

Anne smiled. "They're perfect together, absolutely perfect."

"A match made in heaven."

Anne laughed. "Now you sound like my mother."

\* \* \* \* \*

# Silhouette Intimate Moments®

# COMING NEXT MONTH

## #333 CORRUPTED—Beverly Sommers

Police officer Sandy McGee is on special assignment to protect Johnny Random, a crooked cop. In a world of false identities and misplaced trust, in which even the double-crossers are double-crossed, Sandy, torn between her ethics and her growing passion for Johnny, must choose: honor or love? Or can she have both?

## #334 SOMEONE TO TURN TO— Marilyn Cunningham

Ramsey Delacroix returns to her grandfather's ranch after a shattering divorce. Instead of the safety and reassurance she craves, she finds murder. Compelled to defend her family, yet helpless against her deepening feelings for the bitter Brad Chillicott, Ramsey is forced to choose between loyalty to her family and a dangerous love for a stranger.

## #335 LOVING LIES—Ann Williams

To catch a killer, Lauren Downing finds herself recruited as bait. Working alongside the town's "bad boy," Jesse Tyler, in a race against time, she discovers a deepening passion that goes against all the rules. Despite the odds, they must reveal the killer's identity—will it be in time to save their growing love?

## #336 DREAM CHASERS— Mary Anne Wilson

TV host Jillian Segar, on assignment in volatile South America with her enigmatic former lover Carson Davies, finds herself enmeshed in a web of political intrigue. Irresistibly drawn to Carson, and finding herself falling in love, Jillian must put her life in his hands. Can he be trusted to save her, or will love elude them once again?

## AVAILABLE THIS MONTH:

#329 BETRAYED
Beverly Sommers

#330 NEVER SAY GOODBYE
Suzanne Carey

#331 EMMA'S WAR
Lucy Hamilton

#332 DANGER IN PARADISE
Barbara Faith

**Just when you thought all the good men had gotten away, along comes ...**

# SILHOUETTE Desire

## MAN OF THE MONTH 1990

Twelve magnificent stories by twelve of your favorite authors.

---

In January, FIRE AND RAIN by Elizabeth Lowell
In February, A LOVING SPIRIT by Annette Broadrick
In March, RULE BREAKER by Barbara Boswell
In April, SCANDAL'S CHILD by Ann Major
In May, KISS ME KATE by Helen R. Myers
In June, SHOWDOWN by Nancy Martin
In July, HOTSHOT by Kathleen Korbel
In August, TWICE IN A BLUE MOON by Dixie Browning
In September, THE LONER by Lass Small
In October, SLOW DANCE by Jennifer Greene
In November, HUNTER by Diana Palmer
In December, HANDSOME DEVIL by Joan Hohl

---

Every man is someone you'll want to get to know ... and love. So get out there and find your man!

MOM90-1A

# A BIG SISTER can take her places

She likes that. Her Mom does too.

**HARLEQUIN SUPPORTS BIG SISTERS**
For more information, contact your local Big Brothers/Big Sisters agency.

## BIG BROTHERS/BIG SISTERS AND HARLEQUIN

Harlequin is proud to announce its official sponsorship of Big Brothers/Big Sisters of America. Look for this poster in your local Big Brothers/Big Sisters agency or call them to get one in your favorite bookstore. Love is all about sharing.

BB/BS-1A

You'll flip... your pages won't!
Read paperbacks *hands-free* with

# Book Mate • I

**The perfect "mate" for all your romance paperbacks**
**Traveling • Vacationing • At Work • In Bed • Studying • Cooking • Eating**

Perfect size for all standard paperbacks, this wonderful invention makes reading a pure pleasure! Ingenious design holds paperback books OPEN and FLAT so even wind can't ruffle pages – leaves your hands free to do other things. Reinforced, wipe-clean vinyl-covered holder flexes to let you turn pages without undoing the strap... supports paperbacks so well, they have the strength of hardcovers!

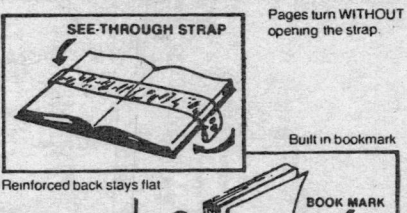

Pages turn WITHOUT opening the strap.

SEE-THROUGH STRAP

Reinforced back stays flat

Built in bookmark

BOOK MARK

BACK COVER HOLDING STRIP

10 x 7¼ opened
Snaps closed for easy carrying, too

Available now. Send your name, address, and zip code, along with a check or money order for just $5.95 + .75¢ for postage & handling (for a total of $6.70) payable to Reader Service to:

Reader Service
Bookmate Offer
901 Fuhrmann Blvd.
P.O. Box 1396
Buffalo, N.Y. 14269-1396

Offer not available in Canada
* New York and Iowa residents add appropriate sales tax.

# Silhouette Romances

# DIAMOND JUBILEE CELEBRATION!

It's Silhouette Books' tenth anniversary, and what better way to celebrate than to toast *you*, our readers, for making it all possible. Each month in 1990, we'll present you with a DIAMOND JUBILEE Silhouette Romance written by an all-time favorite author!

Welcome the new year with *Ethan*—a LONG, TALL TEXANS book by Diana Palmer. February brings Brittany Young's *The Ambassador's Daughter*. Look for *Never on Sundae* by Rita Rainville in March, and in April you'll find *Harvey's Missing* by Peggy Webb. Victoria Glenn, Lucy Gordon, Annette Broadrick, Dixie Browning and many more have special gifts of love waiting for you with their DIAMOND JUBILEE Romances.

Be sure to look for the distinctive DIAMOND JUBILEE emblem, and share in Silhouette's celebration. Saying thanks has never been so romantic....

SRJUB-1

# SILHOUETTE® Desire™
## MAN OF THE MONTH

## SCANDAL'S CHILD
### ANN MAJOR

## When passion and fate intertwine...

Garret Cagan and Noelle Martin had grown up together in the mysterious bayous of Louisiana. Fate had wrenched them apart, but now Noelle had returned. Garret was determined to resist her sensual allure, but he hadn't reckoned on his desire for the beautiful scandal's child.

Don't miss SCANDAL'S CHILD by Ann Major, Book Five in the Children of Destiny Series, available now at your favorite retail outlet.

---

Or order your copy of SCANDAL'S CHILD, plus any of the four previous titles in this series (PASSION'S CHILD, #445, DESTINY'S CHILD, #451, NIGHT CHILD, #457 and WILDERNESS CHILD, *Man of the Month* #535), by sending your name, address, zip or postal code, along with a check or money order for $2.50 plus 75¢ postage and handling for each book ordered, payable to Silhouette Reader Service to:

| In the U.S. | In Canada |
|---|---|
| 901 Fuhrmann Blvd. | P.O. Box 609 |
| P.O. Box 1396 | Fort Erie, Ontario |
| Buffalo, NY 14269-1396 | L2A 5X3 |

Please specify book titles with your order.

SCAN-1A